Praise for
Angie Amalfi Mysteries

"Angie Amalfi is the queen of the culinary sleuths."
— *Romantic Times*

"A winner...Angie is a character unlike any other in the genre."
— *Santa Rosa Press Democrat*

"A tasty treat for all mystery and suspense lovers who like food for thought, murder and a stab at romance."
— *The Armchair Detective*

"Joanne Pence is a master chef."
— *Mystery Scene*

"Pence can satisfy the taste buds of the most skeptical mystery reader."
— *Literary Times*

"Singularly unusual characters...fervently funny."
— *The Mystery Reader*

"A wicked flair for light humor...a delightful reading concoction."
— *Gothic Journal*

"Another terrific book...a bit of Lucille Ball and the Streets of San Francisco"
— *Tales From a Red Herring*

"Murder couldn't be served up in a more delicious manner."
— *The Paperback Forum*

"...the humor, the wit and the satisfying twists of this romantic tale... just the right measures of intrigue, danger, jealousy and warmth."
— *The Time Machine*

Cook's Christmas Capers

Two Angie Amalfi Novellas

Cook's Curious Christmas

&

The 13th Santa

QUAIL HILL PUBLISHING

Quail Hill Publishing
PO Box 64
Eagle, ID 83616

Visit our website at www.quailhillpublishing.net

First Quail Hill Publishing Paperback Printing: December 2013

10 9 8 7 6 5 4 3 2 1

Excerpts copyright © 1993, 1994, 1995, 1996, 1998, 1998, 1999, 2000, 2002, 2003, 2003, 2004, 2006, 2007, 2013
© Can Stock Photo Inc. / lunamarina

ISBN: 0615931847
ISBN-13: 978-0615931845

Cook's
Curious
Christmas

Chapter 1

As ANGELINA AMALFI ENTERED San Francisco's Washington Square, something felt wrong. Usually, even in winter, birds sang, seagulls soared, and flocks of pigeons pecked at the scraps people tossed their way. Now, none were present. While snow and freezing temperatures blanketed most of the country, the weather here was pleasantly cool and crisp. Yet the air was eerily still.

In five days it would be Christmas and she was rushing to the post office to mail presents. Yes, she should have sent them off a week ago, but planning for her wedding was so time-consuming that everything else in her life seemed to be shunted aside, including Christmas.

The Christmas spirit wasn't even a flicker in her heart. This year, the holiday did nothing but create more hubbub and bother than she wanted to deal with.

On top of everything else, she couldn't even find a nearby parking space. Could the parking situation in San Francisco get any worse?

From the corner of her eye she saw a blur. It took a moment to realize it was her friend, Nona Farraday, running by. Truth be told, she and Nona weren't really friends. They had more of a mutual admiration-and-disdain relationship. Angie envied Nona's job as restaurant reviewer and writer for *Haute Cuisine* magazine, and Nona envied Angie's comfortable life and handsome fiancé, San Francisco Homicide Inspector Paavo Smith.

But why, Angie wondered, was Nona in such a hurry?

Angie scanned the direction Nona ran toward. The North Beach park had several areas with trees and bushes. She saw a young man with thick black hair crouching behind an elm. Was Nona looking for him? Who was he? And why, Angie wondered, was he hiding?

Then the trees began to sway.

The earth jolted in sharp side-to-side motions. Angie could barely stay on her feet, and staggered towards a park bench to hold onto the back so she wouldn't fall off her four-inch high heels. A roar filled her head, although she couldn't say if she heard an actual sound or if her eardrums were reacting to power and force and pressure.

The quake didn't stop.

Angie spun around to see some people drop to the ground while mothers captured their children in their arms, holding them close. People's screams matched the sound of the earth.

She was used to sudden rolling tremblers that rattled nerves and little else, and then ended almost as soon as they started. The bad quakes were the ones that went on and on, that continued long enough for a person to wonder, "What will I do if it doesn't stop?" Long enough to see, hear, and feel, the certainties of life crumbling all around.

Angie was young when the last big quake, the Loma Prieta, hit the Bay Area. Only because most people had left work early and were home turning on their TVs to watch baseball's "Bay Bridge World Series," was there relatively little loss of life despite a major freeway collapse and a chunk of the Bay Bridge's upper deck falling to the lower.

That quake seemed to go on forever.

So did this one.

Angie's prayers went immediately to the safety of her family and friends, as well as those around her.

Only a few feet away, two teenage girls huddled together, frozen to the spot, and above them, a tree limb swayed precariously.

"Get away!" The Christmas presents fell from her arms as she grabbed their wrists and pulled. The blond girl cooperated, but the brunette rebelled, and pulled back.

"Let go!" she yelled, twisting away from Angie's hold.

"A branch is about to fall!" Angie screamed. "You've got to run!"

"Leave me alone!"

The girl wouldn't stop fighting. Angie feared she would have to let go for her own safety. "Please," she said, and gave one last, mighty tug.

On the opposite side of San Francisco, Connie Rogers leaned against a counter in her gift shop, Everyone's Fancy. In her thirties, divorced, with blue eyes, short blond hair that curled and fluffed around her face, she didn't see herself so much overweight as "well rounded."

Her store was empty as usual. She had decked the store with Christmas cheer—tinsel, festive lights, a wreath on the door, and even a small tree—but it hadn't helped.

Unless things quickly turned around, she was going to have to sell the business. She hated the thought. She loved her little shop. Each item, be it kitschy knickknacks, pottery, collectibles, or greeting cards, had been chosen with great care. And bought with credit. The interest on the charges was eating her alive. Connie had to be careful with her dollars since she had two mouths to feed—hers and her pound puppy Lily's, who actually wasn't a puppy at all but a five-year old medium-size female with a shaggy cream-colored coat and melt-your-heart big brown eyes.

She went to the door of her shop and opened it wide.

A sudden inexplicable uneasiness gave her the strangest urge to lock the doors, take Lily, and go home. She ignored it and stepped onto the sidewalk. A few cars zipped past. A well-dress man dashed down the street, focused inward, not even noticing her.

The sky seemed unnaturally bright, startlingly so. San Francisco was almost perpetually in a haze of some sort, usually from the cold and fog, rarely from a shimmering heat, and always interlaced with smog of exhaust and industry.

Connie shaded her eyes. A strange energy was in the air. She could almost taste it.

"Lily, come here," she called, suddenly wanting company.

Lily, usually happy to step outside the shop, didn't come.

Connie turned. "Lily?"

The dog stood, but her eyes were wide and questioning. At Connie's urging she took a couple of steps toward the front door, then whimpered and backed away.

At that moment, the building began to sway. The creaking of the wooden walls and floor made a high squeal that was all but drowned out by the clatter of knickknacks knocking about.

Connie spun toward her shop to see Lily crawl under a counter. At the same time some beautiful pottery pieces began to fall. Teetering like a drunken sailor from the force of the quake, she stumbled towards them, hoping to grab the most expensive pieces before they hit the floor and shattered. She would no sooner grab one piece than three more would fall. It was as if some gigantic hand of God shook the shelves. Or considering the damage being done, the Devil.

A shelf unit sprang from the wall, tilting toward Connie. She managed to jump out of the way at the last second as the heavy case crashed to the floor.

Horrified, scared, and heartsick by all that was happening, Connie followed her dog under the counter and hugged Lily tight.

Homicide Inspector Paavo Smith inspected the shriveled, decaying body of an elderly man who had apparently slipped in the bathtub, hit his head, and died.

His partner, Toshiro Yoshiwara, tried not to gag. Yosh was tall for a Japanese with a broad, powerful build. He had recently shaved off all his thick black hair, saying he was sick of his receding hairline and mass of cowlicks.

Paavo looked for bruises or any other sign that the old man's death had not been as natural as the family insisted. No one in that family—a mother, father, their four young children, and the father's two brothers—had noticed that the old man, an uncle to the adult males, was not underfoot. They didn't look for him until he had been dead for five days and the small house, lacking air conditioning, began to smell.

"I've got to get out of here," Yosh said, one hand

holding a handkerchief over his nose, the other pressed to his stomach.

"Go," Paavo told him. "I'll be out in a minute."

Alone now, Paavo looked around the house. He was a tall, broad-shouldered man, with short brown hair, pale blue eyes, pronounced cheekbones and a slight bend to his nose from a long ago break.

The first thing that struck him was that too many people were crammed together in the small three bedroom, two bath house. They claimed that only when they realized none of them had used the smaller bathroom for days—and that no one had seen Uncle Henry—did they find him.

The death was beyond gross incompetency, but was it murder? The family members all said they were simply grateful that Uncle Henry wasn't complaining, causing trouble, or being incontinent.

It wasn't the first time Paavo had seen an old person who had made life difficult for young relatives suddenly become disposable.

A small Christmas tree stood in a corner of the living room. Beneath it were what looked like a truckload of wrapped presents. Paavo wondered if even one was for Uncle Henry.

As soon as the coroner's team bagged the body, Paavo joined Yosh outside.

Despite Paavo's tough cop image, he was glad to get out into the open, to get the taste of death and neglect from his mouth. For some reason, the outside wasn't much better.

The air felt close, heavy, not like San Francisco at all. Usually breezes, if not freezing winds from the ocean, whipped between buildings and nearly blew people out of their shoes.

Not today.

Today, all was still. Unnaturally so. Paavo felt it and looked at Yosh whose wary expression said he, too, was unnerved.

A few cars drove by, but normally adults and children in poorer neighborhoods like this gathered in front of any house with activity, especially if it involved the law. The neighborhood reeked of boredom and despair, but now people stayed indoors.

"Earthquake weather," Paavo said.

Yosh nodded.

Paavo turned to watch as the coroner's team carried the body from the house, followed by the family.

The ground sharply undulated, then shifted to quick side-to-side motions.

Uncle Henry's corpse slid off the gurney onto the street.

The family screamed. The wife began to swoon. Her husband grabbed her arm as he shouted about clumsy city workers, then both stopped in their tracks clutching each other as they felt the quake...and waited for it to stop.

Power lines swayed, and the telephone poles looked like they were made of Jell-O.

Paavo and Yosh pulled the children away from the house into the middle of the street moments before the garage buckled, and the main floor of the house dropped with a sickening crunch.

Stanfield Bonnette opened the door to his refrigerator and his face fell. Stan lived across the hall from Angie. His apartment was smaller; it had a view of the city rather than San Francisco Bay, the bridges and Alcatraz; and his refrigerator was a whole lot emptier.

A slim, somewhat delicate man with the good-fortune of being given a job in a bank through his father's influence, he was often home...and bored...which usually translated into him bothering Angie rather than finding something to do on his own.

She enjoyed cooking and trying out new recipes, and Stan convinced her some time back that if she ate everything she cooked, she would weigh a ton. He, on the other hand, had the sort of metabolism that allowed him to eat and not gain weight.

He could hardly wait for Angie to get back home today. He knew she was fretting about her upcoming wedding, and a nervous Angie cooked to calm herself. What would it be this time? Italian comfort food? Fettuccini with pesto would be good. Or ricotta-filled manicotti. His mouth began to water. Or maybe she would turn to chocolate. A nice chocolate-walnut torte. Or dark chocolate mousse. Or chocolate-filled éclairs. He put his hand on the kitchen counter, ready to swoon with hunger and need.

His eye caught a carton of eggs in the still open refrigerator and he decided to scramble a couple to tide him over for the hour or so it would take Angie to cook up something mouth-watering.

As he reached for the eggs, the carton scooted away from him. Suddenly, the entire refrigerator began to dance from side to side. A quart of milk toppled off the shelf and bounded onto the floor with a wet crash.

Stan clutched the refrigerator for only a moment, then ran to the kitchen doorway and held onto the door jamb. He had been told doorways were the strongest spot in a room.

Tears of fright filled his eyes. "Earthquakes don't go on

this long!" he cried, even though no one was there to hear him. The renovated building had already been through a number of quakes. What if it didn't survive this latest one? What if *he* didn't survive this latest one?

He whimpered.

He heard the wrenching sounds of wood and plaster as it twisted and pulled. Being on the twelfth floor, which was high for a San Francisco apartment building, the sway was perceptible.

The electricity in the apartment crackled then died.

Stan yelped, curled up into a ball, and covered his head with his arms.

Chapter 2

ANGIE OPENED HER eyes. Somehow she had ended up flat on her back.

The two girls had gone. The precariously swaying tree limb hadn't broken off from the trunk after all.

Filled with relief, she sat up.

An old man stood over her. "You okay, miss? Do you need a doctor?"

She did feel a bit woozy, but said, "I'm fine. That was quite a quake! I hope there wasn't much damage."

Children played; mothers huddled in small bunches talking; all seemed unconcerned about what just happened.

"I was in the quake of o-six," the old fellow said. "It was a doozy! I was just a little shaver, mind you, but it's as clear in my head as anything. The fire burned down the whole blooming city, and we all lived in tents for a few weeks."

Angie took his hand as he helped her to her feet. The old boy was nice, but nuts—1906? He was not hundred-years-old plus. In fact, he didn't look a day over eighty.

"Thanks." She picked up her purse. The quake must have been a lot milder than she had thought. "I'm glad everything seems fine."

"Yes," he smiled in toothless splendor. "You'd better get home now. Too much sun, I guess. Are you sure you're all right?"

Something seemed strange, but she couldn't put her finger on what. "Yes, thank you."

Then it struck. Her Christmas packages were gone! Someone must have stolen them while she was passed out. What nerve! What gall! Where was a policeman when you needed one? She would have to report this theft to Paavo, and then go shopping all over again.

First, before anything else, she needed to make sure her fiancé, family and friends were all right. She looked in her purse for her cell phone. Paavo would know if the quake had done much damage elsewhere. Clearly, in North Beach, life was going on as if nothing at all had happened.

Her phone wasn't in her purse. Damn! The thief took that, too. At least her wallet was still there, thank goodness.

As she headed toward her car, she saw a peculiar gathering in a corner of the park. Nearly all the women had long wavy hair. Most wore peasant blouses with jeans or long skirts with paisley or flowery prints. Many wore head scarves of some kind. The men also wore their hair quite long, with flowing shirts or caftans over jeans, and almost all—men and women—wore flat, brown leather sandals. They looked like pictures Angie used to see of the "hippies" that descended on San Francisco years and years ago. *If you're going to San Francisco, be sure to wear some flowers in your hair...*

She remembered her mother singing the old song, and saying hippies weren't nearly so peace-loving or gentle as the song made them seem.

The group was watching some performers dressed up as Commedia dell'Arte characters putting on a show. It must be a revival of some kind. Only in San Francisco, Angie thought. Despite an earthquake, the show must go on.

She hurried back to her car, glad to see no destruction as she went.

When she reached the spot where she had parked her big, new, Mercedes, in its place stood an old-fashioned yellow VW bug—the kind seen in the old-time "Herbie, the Love Bug" movies. Who drove a car like that anymore?

Whoever did had kept it up well. It looked almost new.

Could she be mistaken about where she had parked? She marched up and down the block. Weirdly, all the cars were old. Lots of VWs, lots of tiny little foreign cars, a few behemoth boxy American ones, but not an SUV, Lexus, or even a Ford Taurus in the bunch. How could that be?

But she was sure of where she had parked. She looked for her car keys. They were gone! And her house keys!

Damn! Whoever took her cell phone must have taken her car keys and her car! But how in the world did they know where she had parked?

They would know where her apartment was, however, because they had her car registration!

She only lived a few blocks away at the very top of Russian Hill. To walk there, however, meant hiking up some very steep streets. Still, the thought that someone may have already broken into her apartment, and was stealing her things at that very moment spurred her to dash up the hill in record time.

The front door of the apartment building remained unlocked until late night, and she hurried in, then took the elevator to the manager's apartment on the second floor.

An elderly woman opened the door.

"Mrs. Calamatti!" Angie cried, surprised. Mrs. Calamatti lived on three, not two. She was senile and worried so much about money she often hung around the apartment building's garbage shoot to see if anything valuable was being thrown away. "Is Mr. Anderson in?" Angie asked. "I've lost my key and I need him to let me in my apartment."

"Mr. Anderson?" Mrs. Calamatti repeated. "I don't know any Mr. Anderson. I don't think you live in this building. I know all my tenants."

"*Your* tenants?" The poor woman was even more confused than usual, Angie thought. "They're my father's tenants. He owns the building. You know me, Mrs. Calamatti. Angie Amalfi, apartment 12A. If Mr. Anderson left you in charge, that's fine, but I'd like you to let me into my apartment. I'm afraid someone might try to break into it, or already did!"

"I think you should leave." Mrs. Calamatti looked scared. "You don't live here, and if you persist in disturbing me or my tenants, I'm going to call the police!"

She shut the door. Angie heard the chain snap into place.

She took the elevator up to her apartment.

Before she stepped out, she double-checked that she was on the right floor. The walls were still white, but the carpet had been changed. How odd. She hadn't known it was going be. The hallway was small and probably didn't take long to recarpet, but why in the world did her father pick a rust color? It seemed so dated.

Her apartment door was locked, as it should have been, and there was no sign that anyone was there. Maybe she was in time to save her belongings.

She knocked several times on the door of her neighbor, Stan Bonnette, but he didn't answer.

She paced. If only she had her cell phone, she could call Paavo and tell him what was going on, and then wait in the hallway protecting her apartment.

Just then, the elevator bonged and out stepped Mrs. Calamatti with a police officer.

"I told you to leave the premises," Mrs. Calamatti said. "If you don't go, I'll have you arrested."

Angie looked the young officer in the eye and pointed at her apartment door. "I live there! I don't know what she's told you, but the woman has early Alzheimer's. She's not the building manager. His name is George Anderson. My father owns this building."

"She's crazy," Mrs. Calamatti folded her arms. "And I don't know what she's talking about. I have Alzheimer's what? I'm no thief! She has no business here!"

"I live here! You can ask my neighbor, Stan Bonnette, as soon as he gets back." Angie pointed at Stan's door.

"I don't know who you're talking about!" Mrs. Calamatti shouted.

"Who lives there, then?" Angie shouted back.

Mrs. Calamatti lifted her chin. "That is none of your business!"

"Ladies, stop," the officer said, then faced Angie. "I'm sorry, Miss. I've known Mrs. Calamatti for years and she owns this building. I'm afraid you'll have to leave."

"She's got you fooled!" Angie couldn't believe that the officer had been so easily taken in by the woman. "Call my fiancé, Homicide Inspector Paavo Smith. He'll tell you."

The officer took Angie's arm. "Let's step outside the building, and you can call anyone you like." He nodded at

Mrs. Calamatti as he led Angie onto the elevator. Outside, he told her in no uncertain terms to beat it. Now.

She did, angry and baffled.

Angie "beat it" as far as the corner of the twelve-story apartment building and watched the police officer drive away. Behind her, a narrow walkway along the side of the building led to an area with garbage cans and unfamiliar dumpsters as well as the door to the underground garage.

To her relief, the door was unlocked. Once inside, she took the elevator and then the stairs up to the roof. A separate set of stairs led to her apartment's back door. She had the only apartment in the building with a private roof access. She should get some benefit being daughter to the owner, after all. Strangely, someone had removed the pots of fresh herbs she kept out there. Since she loved cooking, she grew her own basil, parsley, mint, and oregano.

She had hidden an extra key under the basil. It, too, was missing.

She wanted to bang her head against a wall. The bizarreness of her apartment key, cell phone, even her car, all missing, had seemed like a bad joke at first. But when the building manager was also missing, and the police forced her to leave, she got scared. Now, she was just plain angry.

A doormat lay by the back door. It wasn't hers, but it gave her an idea. She peeked under it and sure enough, found her back door key. She unlocked the door.

Relief filled her. Home at last! Finally, all the madness would come to an end.

From the back porch she entered the kitchen.

Only it wasn't her kitchen.

The room began to spin.

Instead of her fire engine red Lacanche professional grade gas range, she eyed a green Kenmore with electric coil burners. She shrank back in horror.

The hanging rack with her All-Clad pots, the wood block that held her Henckels knives, even her Kohler pull-out faucet had vanished.

The dishwasher was no longer a stainless steel Miele, but a Whirlpool. Also green. Why not? It matched the ugly green Frigidaire looking lonely in the spot that once held her large stainless steel freezer-on-the-bottom French-door style Kitchenaid.

She felt as if she was in the middle of an avocado, and she was the pit.

A white generic box, unopened, had "Macaroni & Cheese" in bold black letters. Beside it was a half-eaten bowl of some bizarre concoction that was lumpy and green. She wouldn't feed it to a dog.

Why were these strange foods on her counter...and why was it green Formica when just a few years ago she had installed a beautiful ochre granite?

Was she dreaming? Was she insane? Or was she suddenly a participant in a wildly improbable reality TV show? Rather than *Trading Spaces*, it was *Vanishing Spaces*? Or *American Suic-idol*? Or *Survivor—The "I Lost My Home" Adventure*?

She didn't know what to think, what to do.

On wobbly legs, she stumbled out to the living room. The eight-foot tall, beautiful Douglas fir she had decorated in gold and red ornaments and ribbons was gone, as were all her other Christmas decorations, from the wooden nutcrackers to the stuffed Santa Claus bears to the hand-crafted crèche. Nothing replaced them.

Instead of her beautiful yellow petit point sofa and gorgeous antique Hepplewhite chair, someone had put an L-shaped black Naugahyde monstrosity. It sat on a mustard colored shag rug, and in front of it was a chrome and glass coffee table. A strangled cry fell from her lips.

And the horror got worse.

As she neared the dining area with a black plastic-looking dinette set instead of her solid cherry wood table and chairs, she saw shoes on the ground. Men's shoes.

But they weren't lying flat. They were back on their heels, the toes splayed outward and upward, as if they were still on someone's feet.

She froze. Whose feet? She lived alone. What man would be in her house, lying on her dining room floor, and wearing tastelessly pointy shiny black shoes?

She panted faster than a victim in a slasher movie.

If she thought her legs were wobbly before, they were nothing compared to their state now, as she tiptoed toward the body. It was amazing she could walk at all.

The man was fairly heavy, with receding gray hair. She had no idea who he was.

Her fingers gripped the back of one of the chairs tight. As much as she hated to, she had no choice but to try to find a pulse.

Her hand shook as she slowly reached forward and touched his face. He was cold. Icy cold. No one could be that cold and not be....

She swallowed hard.

She tried to wriggle his finger. It was stiff as a board.

She yanked back her hand and folded her arms tight against her ribs. Who was he? Why was he in her apartment?

And why did he have bright green foam oozing from

the side of his mouth?

Somehow, she managed to cross the room to the end table where she kept her phone, but instead of her such-a-high-gigahertz-number-she-couldn't-even-remember-what-it-was cordless, on the table sat a white "princess" style instrument. One like her mother kept in the bedroom years ago. One with a rotary dial that lit up when the receiver was lifted. One with a short, coiled cord...like a deformed snake...

That did it.

Angelina Rosaria Maria Amalfi ran from her apartment in a complete panic.

Chapter 3

A N UPSET AND SCARED Angie took a remarkably aged taxicab to the Hall of Justice. The driver, when she questioned him, said he heard an earthquake reported as a tiny 2.5 on the Richter scale hit earlier, but nobody felt it. Well, she certainly had!

Angie was accustomed to news delays—everything seemed fine on first report, but only as time went on did the truth come out. The quake was far stronger than reported.

She guessed something strange had happened during the quake. Something that made everything around her feel a little…warped. She shuddered. She was going to find Paavo. He would explain it. He would make everything right again.

The taxi driver never used his cell phone, which was odd. Most cabbies seemed to spend all their time on the phones between talking—hands free, of course—to dispatchers and girlfriends or wives. She asked if she could borrow his phone for a local call, and he acted as if he didn't know what she was talking about.

That was most likely easier for him than out and out refusing. Afraid he wouldn't get a tip, perhaps.

The streets seemed quieter than normal with much less traffic. Only older cars were on the road for some reason, and even the people looked odd. It was as if the street fair that surrounded the performers in Washington Square had spread into a city-wide celebration of ugly old clothes.

She did her best to ignore it. She had bigger things to worry about, like...

No! She refused to think about her apartment or the dead man in it. It must have been a hallucination, a manifestation of her confusion after the earthquake and Mrs. Calamatti's strange behavior.

She wondered if she needed to go to a hospital. But she felt fine...except for seeing things.

She concentrated instead on her missing car, and where in the world poor Mr. Anderson was. Mrs. Calamatti was senile, but she had never been dangerous before. Angie hoped she hadn't gone psycho and hurt the real building manager in her version of the Bates Motel.

Paavo, the most capable, rational man she had ever met in her life, would help her straighten it all out. She felt good just looking at him.

She blinked hard, several times. The George Moscone convention center that took up an entire city block wasn't there. Gone. Vanished. *Nada.*

Impossible! Angie rubbed her forehead. Even if the Moscone Center had been destroyed by the quake, debris would be strewn around. Instead, the space held some old, dilapidated buildings.

Her stomach roiled. Ah! She had it now. She had become confused about the streets, that's all.

She double checked the street signs as they drove by. Okay...someone had moved the signs around. That explained it.

She had been more disoriented by the quake than she realized. It had knocked her over, made her pass out. No wonder everything seemed a little...skewed. What could be more normal?

Her head didn't hurt anywhere. She felt around. She found no bumps.

The taxi stopped and the driver said, "That'll be five-fifty."

She was surprised at how inexpensive the trip was. She handed him a ten.

"Hey! What kind of funny money is this?" He flipped it back and forth, looking at the bill.

What? She looked in her wallet. An old twenty was in there, but everything else had the new hard-to-counterfeit look. The idea that a cab driver didn't recognize her money made something ripple along her back. "Here." She thrust a twenty at him, and jumped out of the cab. "Keep the change!"

She ran into the Hall of Justice. Right in. No one stopped her.

That, also, was too strange for words. Not only were no guards at the entrance, but the metal detectors had been removed. How could that be? Courts were in session. Judges met here. They had to be protected, not to mention the District Attorney and his staff, and even the inspectors like Paavo. They couldn't allow just anyone to walk into the building! What was wrong with these people? She would have complained except she saw no one to complain to.

How weird was this?

Before her, in a corner of the lobby, stood a huge

Christmas tree filled with old-fashioned ornaments, lights, and a manger scene at the bottom. How nice, she thought. Last she had heard, the city wasn't allowing any 'religious' symbols in city buildings. Soft music played "Hark the Herald Angels Sing." If she were a crazy woman, she would think she had traveled through time. But that was impossible.

Still, she felt like a criminal as she walked straight to the bank of elevators without being questioned or having her purse x-rayed to prove she wasn't a terrorist or an assassin. Her heart pounded.

The elevator bonged and the doors opened.

Angie gawked at the short, short skirts of women getting off. And those shoulder pads! Football linemen would be envious. The men's clothes were equally strange. Men working here normally dressed in suits or sports jackets with nice slacks, white shirts and ties, not tie-less leisure suits. What was with all the cheap polyester?

She got on and pushed the button for the fourth floor.

"No Paavo Smith works here!" the receptionist insisted as Angie's head began to ache. She had never seen the woman before, and never wanted to again. She had long curly hair and wore a short paisley dress that looked beyond hideous. And, she was lying. "I've never even heard a name like Paavo. You've got the wrong department!"

"Are you new?" Angie asked. "His partner's name is Toshiro Yoshiwara. Yosh. Surely, you know him."

"No."

"That does it!" Angie marched past the idiotic receptionist and into Homicide, a large room where all the detectives had their own desks, computers, files and bookcases.

A group of strangers looked up at her, startled by her entrance. None of the detectives she knew were there—no Luis Calderon, Bo Benson, Rebecca Mayfield, Bill Sutter, Yosh, or Paavo.

She backed up. Ah! Of course! This wasn't Homicide. The furniture was all wrong. No computers on desks, nothing. How foolish of her! She obviously had gotten off on the wrong floor and was so focused on all the other weird stuff she was seeing, she hadn't noticed her error.

"Sorry," she said. "My mistake." She turned around to leave, but as she did, she saw behind her a wall map of the Bay Area with red circles and dates on it. Tacked up beside it were letters printed in a strange hand. The one nearest Angie began with, *This is the Zodiac speaking. I like killing people.*

Angie gasped.

The Zodiac was a serial killer who had terrorized the Bay Area from the late 1960's to the mid-1970s. If Angie was remembering her San Francisco history correctly—she was a bit of a local history buff and had even taught a couple of community courses on it—the Zodiac was never caught, and his identity never determined.

Most law professionals assumed he had died, moved away, or ended up in an insane asylum. So, Angie wondered, massaging her throbbing temples, why was information about him on the wall now? Had some news broken in the case? But more importantly, it meant this room *was* Homicide.

She spun back, her pulse racing.

"You really must leave, miss," the receptionist said.

Just then, another woman walked into the room.

Angie stared in shock. She recognized her best friend,

Connie Rogers, who should have been working at her gift shop. Instead, she strolled into Paavo's workplace and boldly sat down at Luis Calderon's desk.

Angie couldn't believe her eyes. She had never seen her friend that way. First, instead of her short, light blond hair, it was much darker—her natural color, most likely— much longer and worn in layers that flipped outward. It reminded Angie of someone...

Then she remembered. Not long ago, Hollywood released a movie adapted from "Charlie's Angels," an old TV show. She had read stories about Farrah Fawcett on the original show and how her hairdo had become the style for a nation.

Connie should not be wearing Farrah Fawcett hair. It looked hideous on her.

But more remarkable than the hair or the too-thick eyeliner, were her clothes. She was wearing an SFPD uniform. What the hell was going on?

"Connie!" Angie rushed to her. "Where's Paavo?"

"I'm sorry," the receptionist said to Connie. "She just burst in here asking for someone named Paavo Smith. I'll call security."

"It's okay, Georgia. I know Paavo Smith," Connie said, eying Angie as if she were a stranger. "Why are you looking for him here?"

"He works here!"

Connie's eyes narrowed. "Did he tell you that? Trying to impress you, I suppose. Paavo Smith definitely does not work here."

Angie ran her fingers through her hair. "Connie, what the hell is going on? It's as if everyone's in on some kind of joke except me!"

"How do you know my name?" Connie's expression

turned hard and unbelievably forceful...for Connie.

Instead of answering the foolish question, Angie demanded, "Why are you wearing that uniform?"

Connie smoothed her shirt. "I'm on detail here, not plainclothes yet. And I'm proud of this uniform!"

"You're on detail?" The words caught in Angie's throat.

"What's wrong with that? Women can handle homicide as well as any man, and I'll prove it."

"Of course they can! Rebecca Mayfield proves it every day," Angie shouted.

"Who?"

Angie could stand no more, and ran out of the bureau.

This all had to be some awful joke. Some "let's make the bride think she's nuts" kind of a joke that all her friends were taking part in.

Well, she hated to tell them, but they were doing a much better job than they ever expected. She had visions of a rubber room in her future.

Paavo Smith shut his eyes and, in hopes of clearing his mind, spoke aloud one of the personal mantras he had been given by a disciple of the Maharishi Mahesh Yogi. *"Shri angh namah namah."* He took a deep breath on a count of three, held it, released it on a count of five, and then opened his eyes again.

The crazy woman before him looked as insane as ever, but now she was staring at him as if he was the one who had lost his mind. He held out his hands to her, and in a soft, hushed voice said, "You must calm yourself. Tell me the name of your doctor."

She socked him in the arm. It hurt!

They stood in his doorway. He had been suffering with another of his migraines, and was lying on a futon with a banana peel draped across his forehead, when he heard the insistent ringing of his doorbell and pounding on the door. He opened it to find a very attractive woman who shouted, "Paavo!" then threw herself into his arms babbling about an earthquake, about the world going insane, about his disguise—*what disguise?*—and wondering what she should do.

When he simply asked her who she was, she burst into tears.

He peeled her off him and studied her. Frankly, he wished he could place her because she was stellar, but she was a stranger to him.

Her brown hair was cut much shorter than most women wore, and it had gold streaks in it. Her skirt was a strange style that hung straight and then flared out at the bottom, and reached all the way down to her knees as if she were an old lady rather than someone who looked like she was born for mini-skirts. Besides that, she seemed to have on two tops, both stretchy and fitted close to her skin. The outer had a deep scoop-neck, and the under garment covered up some of the plunging cleavage. Which was a shame, in his opinion.

At least her platform shoes were stylish, although he had never seen ones quite like hers.

He glanced down at his own shiny Florsheims with their inch-high heels. Now, those were shoes!

"Not you, too!" She wiped away her tears. Her voice caught as she lamented, "What's happened to you, Paavo? What's happened to the world?"

The world? His mind raced. Maybe she was a peacenik who was sure the US, Soviet Union and Red China would blow each other up. That the Cold War would become hot had been predicted for a long time, Vietnam notwithstanding.

He dropped his hands, feeling somewhat foolish when he realized he had been standing there with them dangling in the air. "You're scaring me, miss. How do you know my name?"

"How?! We're..." She stopped speaking.

He leaned back. "We're what?"

Her soulful brown eyes looked so pleadingly at him, he wanted to say something to help her, but he had no idea what that would be. "I'm sorry, miss, but you must have me mixed up with someone else."

"Don't call me miss! My name is Angie. I'm Angie!" She was growing hysterical again as she shouted her name at him. She seemed to expect it to mean something. It didn't.

The neighbors would be coming out any minute the way she was shrieking. "You've got to chill!" he said.

"What?"

That surely didn't work. "Where's your home?" he asked softly.

"Russian Hill," she murmured, then shook her head. "This has got to be a dream." She gazed up, her pain evident. "It's one of those dreams that feels very real. You have those, too, don't you, Paavo?"

Her familiarity with him, her ease despite being a complete stranger, troubled him. It made him want to help her, to protect her...and the last thing he needed was another woman in his life. Especially such a pretty one. "I'm sorry, miss. Did we meet at some party, maybe?"

Her eyes widened. "You hate parties!"

"Now I know you've got me mixed up with someone

else. I love parties."

As she gawked at him, her hands curled into little fists. She had already hit him once. Was she violent as well as crazy? He stepped back.

"This simply isn't funny, Paavo! It's no joke! If anything, it borders on cruel."

What in the world is she talking about? Strangely, she sounded so convincing, it made him want to believe her. But he couldn't. "I don't know what's wrong, miss, but this is no joke."

"Angie, I said! My name is Angie." She drew in her breath. "The last thing that made any sense to me was the big earthquake."

"Big earthquake?" he murmured. The last big earthquake that hit San Francisco was in the 1950's! This poor young woman really was battier than a loon. He would have to humor her. "Sure, the earthquake." He gave her a dopey smile.

Alice in Wonderland falling down a rabbit hole, stepping through a looking glass, or both, had nothing on her, Angie thought, as she looked at the ridiculously smiling stranger who was also her fiancé.

She pinched herself and could feel it. Did it hurt when one pinched oneself in a dream?

This didn't feel like a dream, though. Had the earthquake left her mad? Or could it be—she swallowed hard—that she'd been killed in the quake? That she was dead? If so, was this heaven? Actually, considering the way Paavo looked with his long, fluffy hair, sideburns that resembled bacon slabs, a mustache that would make a walrus proud, and wearing plaid polyester slacks and a shiny blue shirt, it was probably The Other Place.

Yet, she stood on the doorstep of his house. She had taken a bus to get here—her coins worked in the fare box.

Paavo lived in an old bungalow in the outer Richmond district not far from the Pacific Ocean. It wasn't elegant enough to be called a "Craftsman," but was simply a little one bedroom, one bath cottage, like so many in this area that had been inexpensively built around the 1930's. She came here out of desperation, although she hadn't expected him to be home. He usually worked until late at night on his cases, yet here he was.

Tears filled her eyes. "Paavo, it's me, Angie. Angie Amalfi. Surely that means something to you."

"Amalfi?" If he were a cartoon, a light bulb would be shown above his head. "I know!"

"Yes?" Hope filled her.

"It's a place in Italy! The Amalfi coast. I've heard of it!" He frowned. "I've never been there, though. Never been out of the States, as a matter of fact. I was one of the lucky ones. My number didn't come up in the draft."

What draft? She put her hand to her chest to calm her racing heart. "May I use your phone to call my father? Maybe he can make sense of all this. I'd use my cell, but it's missing."

"Your cell?" He took a step back. "You live in a cell? What...what kind of cell?"

He warily eyed her as if he thought her cell must be padded. "Of course I don't live in a cell! I live in an apartment, or"—she thought about her apartment—"I did."

Her breathing grew faster and the world started to flash black and purple spots before her eyes. What was happening to her, to her family, to her fiancé?

Somewhere on the street, she began to hear music—a saxophone—playing a slow, mournful rendition of "Beyond the Sea."

Paavo was talking to her, she saw his lips moving, but she stopped hearing his words. A loud wail filled her ears...and it took a moment to realize the sound came from her mouth. A loud, long cry of desperation. A moment later, the world went mercifully black.

Angie opened her eyes to find Paavo's arms around her waist as he half-dragged, half-carried her into the house. "I'm sorry, miss," he kept saying over and over, along with, "What are the neighbors going to think?"

Since when did Paavo care about his neighbors?

He dropped her onto a chair...or sort of chair. It was a navy-blue bean bag monstrosity. It was all she could do not to roll right off. Somehow, she managed to sit up.

It was Paavo's living room...but wasn't. "Where's your furniture?"

Wide frightened eyes, darted left and right. "It's...uh...all around you?"

"No! Your big sofa and overstuffed arm chairs. Your TV, VCR, DVD, PC, MP-3—"

"Miss, I don't know what you're talking about."

"Angie!" she shouted. "My name is Angie!"

He took a deep breath before continuing. "My guru says the best thing one can do is rid oneself of possession and find a quiet spot to meditate." He gestured toward a Japanese wall scroll. Beneath it was a large black rock and a gray pottery bowl filled with water. "I use the *tokonoma*, water and earth as my personal resting place."

Angie was sure she would need a personal resting

place—an eternal one—if she didn't get to the bottom of this nonsense and soon.

Slowly, her gaze drifted over his living room. She gawked at a fake Christmas tree made out of what looked like aluminum foil. It held a few blue ornaments. On the floor, a color wheel with green, red, yellow and blue plastic filters faced it. At least it wasn't switched on and rotating.

An olive green shag rug covered the floor...what was with all the shag rugs? Bean bag chairs and enormous pillows as furniture. A low, square coffee table. Blue beads covering the doorway between the living room and kitchen. Boards and cinder blocks for a bookcase, and weirdest of all, large, strange posters on the wall with people she didn't recognize in odd costumes. One said *Sock it to me!* and the other, *Here come da judge!* She guessed they meant something, but she surely didn't know what.

"Let me get you some water," Paavo said, escaping to his kitchen.

She drew in her breath and waited for him to return.

"Connie, it's me." She heard Paavo's voice softly speak, and then drop even further.

He was talking to Connie!

Please, please, please make all this madness be an evil, rotten, I'll-never-forgive-them joke.

She crept to the door to hear better. Paavo was whispering. "I don't think she's actually crazy, just confused. I'm not sure what to do with her. She acts like she knows me. She almost has me believing I'm the one who's lost his mind."

Angie pressed her hand to her mouth.

"Bad acid?" Paavo asked. "She doesn't look like a doper."

Acid? Angie's eyes rounded like dinner plates. Wasn't

that some kind of 1960's psychedelic drug? She had never paid much attention to her parents' generation.

"Okay," Paavo continued. "I'll keep you posted. I'm getting her some water."

Angie scooted back to the beanbag chair, but as she passed the coffee table, she saw a stack of newspapers on the floor.

The top headline read, "Ford Greets Soviet Premier." Ford? Who was that? The only famous Fords she could think of were Henry and Harrison.

She picked up the newspaper...Gerald Ford. She shuddered. Gerald Ford was president before she was even born.

There was another headline about the upcoming Patty Hearst trial. Patty Hearst was more familiar to her than Gerald Ford, but not by much.

Her eye jumped to the masthead and the date...*San Francisco Chronicle*...December 17, 1975.

Her body went cold.

She picked up an earlier newspaper in the pile. December 16, 1975. And the one before that, and before that. All were dated that same week.

The spots that had jumped before her eyes earlier began to do their dance again. She fell into the beanbag chair and took deep breaths.

I can't faint. I can't faint. Please, God, let me wake up from this nightmare!

Holding a water glass straight out in front of him as if he were afraid she would turn into a snake and strike, Paavo walked toward her. *He does think I'm insane!* At that moment, she realized she had to be careful not to give him any excuse to cart her off to a sanitarium...or whatever they used back in 1975. Did they do lobotomies back then?

The dark spots began to form once more.

She gripped the water glass with two hands. "You didn't have to put it in a glass. The bottle would have been fine."

"Bottle?" he asked. "You mean...you want liquor?"

"Liquor? No!" She bit her bottom lip. "No, I mean a water...nothing." She took a sip. "Ooooh...tap water. Umm. Yum. Nice. Very nice."

His expression turned even more quizzical. She took another tiny sip. She lived in the twenty-first century; she knew all about the impurities in city water. Although, come to think of it, she hadn't heard of people dropping like flies from tap water back before bottled water became the rage. She leaned forward and picked a newspaper off the floor, put it on the coffee table, and held the water glass hovering over it. "You don't mind if I put this on the paper?" She hoped he would tell her it was a rare, old copy.

"No. I've read it already."

"That's what I was afraid of," she whispered, putting the glass down.

"What?"

"Nothing." She smiled at him. "I couldn't help but overhear you mention the name Connie. Was that Connie Rogers?"

His eyebrows rose. "Uh...yes....She remembered you asking about me at Homicide, and she thinks this—you being here—is my fault. But I swear I never met you before! I'd remember you. Trust me on that."

Angie leaned forward, elbow to knee, chin to hand, which wasn't an easy thing to do in a beanbag chair. She was half curled into a pretzel already. "Do you work with her?"

He bristled. "I'm no pig!"

It took Angie a moment to close her mouth, swallow hard, and then force out, "What do you do?"

"I'm a teller at the B of A."

"*Oh, my God!*"

"Criminy sakes, it's not that bad!"

If she had a fan, she would be fluttering it in front of her face right then. The air had gone way too still. She slowly stood. "I...I'd like to use your bathroom if I may..."

"Sure, it's..."

He stopped talking as she headed down the hallway. She locked the door, and leaned back against it. Her whole world, everything she knew and loved, had all changed.

She felt as if she was living a combination of *The Wizard of Oz* and the old British (and American copied) TV show, *Life on Mars*. And she hated it!

Why was she here?

And how was she ever going to make things right again?

This was madness. People don't simply wake up one day and find themselves some forty years in the past! But it wasn't really the past.

Paavo was here.

And Connie.

But they weren't the Paavo and Connie that she knew. The thought struck that perhaps no one was anyone she knew. They might look familiar, but they weren't.

The only one who's the same is me.

What a frightening concept that was.

She could feel hysteria bubbling up, threatening to take over.

She splashed cold water on her face. She simply had to play along. Make everyone think she was fine.

But her apartment wasn't hers any longer.

And a dead man was inside it.

"Oh, no!" she wailed, then clamped her hand tight over her mouth, staring at the door and hoping Paavo didn't hear her.

Don't panic!

She really, really wanted to panic, however.

"Angie?" Paavo called. "Are you all right?"

"Yes, sweet—, I mean, yes. I'll be right there."

With a firm resolve not to say or do anything that might give Paavo reason to call the men with white coats and straitjackets, she left the bathroom and sauntered into the living room.

It was empty.

She heard Paavo in the kitchen.

The kitchen was surprisingly familiar. Its tall cream-colored cabinets with red hardware, white tile, and white appliances hadn't been remodeled for decades. The stove and refrigerator were even older than the ones she knew.

Paavo was putting coffee grounds into a clear glass percolator. She hadn't seen one of those since the last time she was in an antique store.

He glanced up and gave a wary smile. "Better?"

"Yes. Much." She sat down at the kitchen table. It was gray and white Formica with matching chairs. At least it wasn't avocado green.

His phone rang. She watched in stunned shock as he went to the wall and picked up a phone that had a cord attached to it.

A cord?

"Nona, calm down," he said.

Nona? Nona Farraday? Why is she calling him? He scarcely knows her.

"Nona, baby, it's all right. I'll be down there. I'll take

care of it."

Baby!? Paavo never called anybody baby—not her, and certainly not Nona! Yuck! Now she knew she was crazy.

He faced her. "I've got to go down to City Jail. My friend Nona is being questioned. Her chef was found dead near her house, poisoned, and she's super freaked out about it."

Angie stood, trying to overlook Paavo's weird use of 'super.' And 'freaked out.' "Are you talking about Nona Farraday?"

He stared. "You know Nona as well?"

"Of course! And she's my friend, not yours!"

Paavo looked at her as if she was even crazier. "How can you say that? She's my girlfriend! I love her!"

Angie gaped. This was not Paavo! This was not her fiancé!

In a complete panic, she blindly ran out the door and down the street.

Chapter 4

PERHAPS BECAUSE THE old song "Beyond the Sea" was going through her head, without thinking about it, Angie turned towards the Pacific Ocean. Land's End, a narrow park along the water's edge, wasn't far from Paavo's home. It seemed like a good place to think.

The park she knew had signs, monuments, and people. But now she found an empty parking lot that led to an unpaved pathway skirting wild and rocky cliffs facing the ocean. She walked along the path, and after a while left it. Out on the headland she watched the tide splash against the rocks far below.

This, at least, was familiar to her. The ocean and the landscape around it were immutable. What could a mere earthquake do to them? The Golden Gate Bridge looked the same as ever. The Farallon Islands were off-shore and only visible on the clearest of days. The little blip of a quake in the earth's crust hadn't mattered to them at all. She held onto the view like a beacon of sanity in a world gone mad.

In the distance, a saxophone played a slow, plaintive song. An old song, familiar...

She followed the music. Deep into the park she saw the

sax player sitting on some rocks a few feet from the walkway.

The words to the song came to her. *"If I could save time in a bottle..."*

How did she know that? She didn't remembering knowing the song or its syrupy words. How could the words come to her now?

She must have made a noise or something, because the musician abruptly stopped playing, turned, and looked at her.

"Hello," he called, scrambling to his feet. "What a surprise to see you. I hope I didn't disturb your visit to the park today."

He was a middle-aged man, overweight, with graying blond hair combed straight back from his forehead, and heavy black-rimmed glasses.

"You didn't disturb me," she said. "I was enjoying it. I didn't mean for you to stop."

"It's okay. Now I have a chance to wish you a very nice day." He bobbed his head as he spoke, his voice low.

He seemed somewhat mentally challenged. "You play very well," she said with a smile.

He stepped a bit closer. "Did you feel the earthquake?"

"Oh, my God! You felt it, too?" Elation filled her. Was she back to her world? Her time? Had she finally awoken from a bizarre nightmare?

"Yes. Of course. I hope my mother's all right. She lives in Santa Rosa. I wanted to call her but there's no pay phone around here. I think she might be worried about me."

Oh, dear. "You need to find one because you don't have a cell phone, right?" she asked hopefully.

"A what?"

Her thin hope crashed. "Nothing."

"Can you play the saxophone?" He lifted it high. "You can borrow mine if you want."

"I don't play."

"It's not hard. Not if I can do it. I was in the war, you know."

"Vietnam?"

"No. I was in Korea. I flew a plane." He stretched out his arms and ran in circles like a little kid playing "airplane." When he stopped, he stood beside her. He was a surprisingly large man up close. Much taller and broader of shoulder than she expected.

For some reason, she felt uneasy, and tried to brush it off. If he was once a pilot, he had to have been quite bright and sharp before the war did this to him. "That's very good," she said, forcing a smile. "You must be proud."

"My name's Tim Burrows." He played a quick riff of notes on his sax, and she smiled. "What do you do?" he asked.

She nearly said "nothing" since all her recent attempts at a job had been colossal failures. "A little of this, a little of that."

"That sounds very important." His gray eyes were small under thick glasses. "I don't have a job. People won't hire me. I have a plate in my head, and sometimes it makes it hard to think. People say it happened to me because I was in the Air Force and I killed people. Everybody hates the military. They say I got what I deserved." He looked puzzled. "Maybe so."

Angie was horrified. "I'm sorry that's been your experience."

"You're a nice lady."

Lady...there was an old fashioned word no one used anymore. "Thank you," she said. "I'd better get going.

Good-bye, now!"

She started to walk away along the path.

"Have a nice day!" he called, and soon after started playing "Sittin' on the Dock of the Bay." It made her smile. How could he have worried her?

She was only about half way back when she saw Paavo approach. Not the real Paavo, but the leisure-suited, long-haired, mustachioed interloper who had taken the place of the man she loved.

"How did you find me?" she asked when they met.

"It wasn't too difficult. When you ran off, I was tempted to let you go, but then I started to worry about you. I saw you turn west toward the ocean and decided to come looking. I didn't want to hear that you reached the water and kept on going!"

She shuddered at the image his words conveyed. "No, I should think not. But you really don't have to worry about me. I know I'm nothing to you." She turned away from him.

"Angie!" he called.

She didn't want to face him and hurried ahead.

"Are you sure you're all right?" Paavo asked, catching up quickly.

No! I'm not! She pivoted in the opposite direction from him, leaving the path and blindly rushing into the shrubbery that lined it. As she did, her eye caught something blue and pointy under a bush. She recognized the odd shape and stopped, staring.

"What is it?" Paavo asked.

She pointed. It looked like the heel of a woman's shoe. She flashed back to her apartment, to finding a man's body....

Paavo pushed aside some of the brush. "My God!" He

grabbed Angie's arm and roughly spun her around. "Don't look!" he said, then lurched into some shrubs a few feet away and threw up.

Angie stared in shock. Paavo never threw up. "Ol' iron guts," his homicide partner, Yosh, called him.

"Paavo?" she whispered.

"There's so much blood and.... She was stabbed, I think." His face was white; his hands shook. "Let's get the hell out of here!"

"Wait! No! We've got to call the police."

"No way. The bacon boys don't like me and I don't like them. Besides, this has nothing to do with us." He grabbed her hand. "Come on!"

Open-mouthed, she gaped, barely comprehending what she'd just heard. "Paavo, the woman was murdered!"

"Yeah, and when the cops show up, they'll question us. You act like you hardly know your own name. How will you answer their questions?"

He was right.

He half dragged her back to the parking lot. "I'm calling Connie Rodgers. She'll know how to keep us out of this. It's not like we've ever been involved with any other murders, right?"

Uh, oh! "Paavo," Angie said meekly.

"Yes?"

She cleared her throat. "When you tell Connie about this dead body"—Angie swallowed hard, realizing how bad her next words were going to sound—"I've got some additional rather hard-to-believe information you ought to give her."

Chapter 5

CONNIE ROGERS STOOD in the apartment Angie Amalfi claimed was hers and looked at the body on the floor.

She didn't know how anyone ever became accustomed to this job. This was her fifth dead body since being detailed to Homicide, and it hadn't gotten any easier. Three of them had died at home, the causes quickly determined to be natural. The fourth was a little kid who had choked on a toy. She would never forget that heartbreaking case. And now this.

The medical examiner inspected the corpse and declared the man had been poisoned. Maybe he concluded that because of the green foam around the man's mouth, but she couldn't be sure.

In fact, she didn't think she wanted to know, which wasn't a good idea for someone who hoped to become a homicide inspector. It was the highest rung in the Bureau of Inspectors, the area that good cops with a talent for analysis and stick-to-itiveness aspired to. But the thought of homicides made her stomach flip-flop.

When the coroner began muttering something about rigor mortis, Connie felt so woozy she went into the den.

A retired professor of sociology, Aloysius Starr, rented the apartment. A driver's license photo as well as the apartment manager, Rosa Calamatti, identified him as the dead man. He had no known relatives in the area.

The den was filled with his books, and on the desk sat an IBM Selectric with the little metal balls that bounced around and around as you typed, and you could easily pop one out and drop a new one in to change the font. Connie had wanted one until she saw the price.

She opened the middle drawer of the victim's desk and saw a stack of business cards in one corner. The first card in the stack was that of Alan Trimball, chef at Nona's, A Restaurant. Connie hated the pretentious sound of "a restaurant" tacked onto the name. What else should it be? A horse food factory?

The chef's name, however, seemed familiar.

With gloves on, she picked up the phone and called Bruce Whalen, the homicide inspector who was assigned to mentor her. "It's Connie. What was the name of your murdered chef?"

"Alan Trimball. Why?"

As Connie explained where she was, and told him about the corpse before her, his question echoed in her head. *Why?* The two men apparently knew each other, and now both were dead.

Why?

"Oh, no!" Paavo wailed as he put down the phone. Angie had never heard her fiancé wail before. She had to admit it was more than a little annoying. She was waiting to hear from Connie who was investigating the body in

Angie's apartment at the same time as two of the more senior inspectors—two men Angie had never heard of—went to Land's End.

Listening to Paavo, however, it was clear he wasn't talking to Connie.

"What's wrong?" Angie asked as soon as he hung up the phone.

"Nona's been arrested," he said. "Poor baby!"

Baby...again! Angie fumed, arms crossed. "So, what are you going to do? Bail her out?"

"I'm not sure she can be bailed out. Not for a while, anyway, according to her attorney. He said she's going to have to go through an arraignment. The case is serious—double homicide."

"Double homicide? What are you saying?"

"It was her cooking that killed both Alan Trimball and Professor Starr—that's the name of the dead man in what you say is your apartment." He quickly told Angie all he had learned about Aloysius Starr and about Nona's chef being found dead a short distance from her home.

Angie couldn't believe what she was hearing. "Her cooking is fairly hideous, but it is not fatal. Are you saying Nona knew Professor Starr, too?"

"That's the thing. She claims she doesn't. But her food killed him. It was her recipe for boiled Brussels sprouts, black soy beans, and tofu, all mashed together. According to Connie, the food was laced with arsenic. The murders are connected, and Nona is the prime suspect."

"What are you going to do?" Angie asked. She didn't like Nona, but Nona was no killer. Well, that might not be true. Nona in her lifetime wasn't a killer. This Nona, she had no idea of...and that recipe did sound lethal.

"Nona asked me to keep her restaurant going until she

gets this cleared up. It's the least I can do for her." Paavo sat down and ran his hands through his long, wavy hair. "But how I'm supposed to it with her cook dead and Nona in prison, I have no idea. I wonder if the dishwasher can cook. Or one of the waiters? Do you think customers would notice if I bought a bunch of TV dinners?"

"What kind of food does she serve?" Angie asked.

"Macrobiotic," Paavo said. "Lots of brown rice, barley, millet, tofu, and vegetables. Not a prime rib or thick steak to be found. The truth is, I don't much care for it."

That, Angie thought, was the most sensible thing he had said yet. "Tell you what. You get some of her favorite recipes for this macrobiotic food from Nona, and I'll cook them."

"You will? Do you know how?"

"More than you'll ever imagine. In fact, since I haven't eaten anything much since I've gotten here, why don't I cook you something you'll really like, my carbonara with prosciutto dish, for example?"

"I don't think I've ever eaten prosciutto. It's Italian ham or bacon, right?"

"Ham. Bacon is pancetta. Trust me, you'll love this dish. You always have."

Chapter 6

ANGIE WENT WITH Paavo to Nona's, A Restaurant and helped him put up signs saying the restaurant would reopen the next night. Christmas lights had been strung around the front entrance, and a small Santa statue sat by the cash register. The dining area was fairly small, with eight tables set up for four people at each. The kitchen was also small, with aged but adequate appliances, although Angie realized that everything looked aged to her these days.

As Paavo walked aimlessly around trying to figure out what to do, Angie went through the macrobiotic menu to see what she needed to prepare. She was appalled. How did Nona expect to make any money off this so-called food? To forbid the use of butter, cream, cheese, eggs—not to mention meat or fish—or anything else that raised recipes from merely adequate to great, made no sense to her whatsoever.

She tossed the menu and came up with her own ideas. She remembered a time, early in her relationship with Paavo, when she had to deal with macrobiotic food at a bed and breakfast. She had managed to work with it then, and she could do so again.

Spices were her friend, and she wrote down ideas for curries using coconut milk to make the sauce creamy. White rice was frowned on, but brown wasn't very tasty in her opinion. She decided to offer customers a choice of jasmine rice or na'an...let their conscience be their guide.

Along with the curries, she planned dishes with chopped vegetables, peppers, onions, and garlic sautéed in olive oil, using a variety of seasonings—some Italian, some Mexican, some Chinese. With the Italian, she would serve homemade bread with little plates of olive oil and balsamic vinegar; with the Mexican, steamed tortillas; and no matter what Nona thought, white rice with the Chinese.

She was creating her own menu when a good-looking, tall, svelte, age twenty-something man walked in. He had thick brown hair, combed to sweep luxuriously back from his brow, and piercing navy blue eyes. Paavo introduced him as Lorenzo McCaffrey, one of Nona's two waiters.

"I came by to see if the place was open, or if somebody was here who needed help," Lorenzo said.

"That was thoughtful," Angie told him as Paavo went off to the dining room. She explained about the menu and her role in the restaurant, and then she said, "I'm sorry to hear about your chef's murder. It must be hard to deal with. Were you close to Alan Trimball?"

He shrugged. "Not really."

"Did he ever mention Professor Aloysius Starr?"

"Starr? No, not that I recall." He took out the flatware and began polishing it to wipe away water spots.

"Did Nona talk about Starr?" Angie put down her pen.

"No. Why do you want to know that? Who's Starr?" Lorenzo rubbed the fork tines until they shone.

"He was a sociology professor at U.C. Berkeley. I

thought Alan might have mentioned him, that's all."

"Oh...yeah, well Alan did study sociology at Berkeley, but I don't remember him saying much about it."

Angie was surprised to hear that. "He went to U.C. Berkeley?"

"He did." Lorenzo shut the drawer with the flatware and faced her. "Alan used to say that if he'd been smart instead of ethical, he could have made a fortune after college."

"Really?" Angie was surprised. Sociology was hardly a high-paying field. "Doing what?"

"He never said, but he would look at Nona and say she threw away her money, and then shake his head."

"What did he mean?"

"I'm not sure. She had gone away for a week to some self-help seminar and it really set Alan off. I guess he thought it was a stupid way to spend a vacation, but maybe there was more to it than that." He put on his jacket, ready to leave.

"Self-help?" She tried to remember what she had heard about those times. Was EST of that period? She wasn't even sure what EST meant, come to think of it.

"ISMI," Lorenzo said, heading towards the door.

"Is me? What's me?" Angie asked, going after him.

"No, not is me, I.S.M.I. It's pronounced 'is me.' But really, where have you been? Everyone knows about it. The Individual System for Meaning Institute. Hell, it's put Mendocino on the map! That's where Nona went for her vacation."

Angie was about to ask him more questions when the restaurant's phone rang. Lorenzo left as Paavo answered it.

He quickly handed the receiver to Angie. "It's the police," he said. "They want to question you. Right now."

oOo

Angie sat in Homicide's interview room. Across the table from her were Connie and Homicide Inspector Bruce Whalen. Whalen looked like he was in his late thirties or early forties, somewhat stocky, with thinning black hair. He was a plain man, but Angie suspected he was an okay guy...when he wasn't treating you like a potential murderer.

"There must be some reason why you thought that was your apartment," Bruce repeated for the tenth time.

"I don't know what more to tell you." Angie held her head. How many ways could she say the same thing? "It just seemed like it was. I have no idea why. As I said, I must have some bizarre type of amnesia."

"Probably brought on by the trauma of having killed a man!" Bruce shouted.

"I didn't kill anybody."

His gaze was hard and unflinching. "First, you and your friend, Paavo Smith, report finding a body out at Land's End. Now we will admit that it appears to be the work of the Zodiac—the multiple knife wounds...and other things...his MO all the way. But the real question is, why were *you* the one to find it? And then, you just happen to mistakenly think you live in an apartment where another person is found dead. What are you, a corpse magnet? Few people find one dead body in an entire lifetime, and you find two within hours of each other."

"I can't explain it!" Angie cried. "I'm not even supposed to be here! None of this makes any sense to me!"

"Which sounds like you're already trying to build an insanity defense. Well, let me tell you, that 'I'm crazy' stuff doesn't work in this city!"

"But 'I ate too many Twinkies' does?" she said with a

sneer, thinking of the infamous Twinkie defense when City Superintendent Dan White shot and killed Mayor George Moscone and gay-activist City Superintendent Harvey Milk.

Her interrogator frowned. "What?"

Oops, wrong time period. "Nothing," Angie said. Dan White ended up getting only two years for the two assassinations based on the defense of "the sugar in Twinkies made me do it," and San Francisco juries have been a laughing stock ever since. But the world has a way of righting wrongs, and Dan White took his own life not long after being released from prison.

"Let's go outside," Bruce said to Connie.

A chill went from down from Angie's spine. What did they want to discuss that couldn't be said in front of her?

Connie was glad to see the questioning stop. She had no idea why, but she actually felt sorry for Angelina Amalfi. The woman seemed nice, but terribly confused.

The coroner had said that judging from the state of Aloysius Starr's body, he had been dead more than twenty-four hours, which put his death a few hours after Alan Trimball's. The manager of the apartment building remembered Angie from earlier that afternoon. Mrs. Calamatti had turned her away, but obviously Angie had found a way to get inside through the roof.

How did she know the apartment had a roof access? She must have been there before.

Connie faced Bruce, "What do you think?"

"I think it's amazing that she seems so believable," he said. "Except that she's obviously hiding something from us. If it weren't for that, I'd say let her go. She's a confused woman who seems to either not know or not remember Aloysius Starr or anything about him. The problem with that is, why, out of all the apartments in the city and county that she could have gone to, did she choose his? It's got to be that she *does* know him, has been to his apartment in the past, and is either a top-notch actress or something bad happened to her that wiped out her memory."

"The latter makes sense." Connie said. "She doesn't seem like a killer."

"Not that most killers 'seem like' killers," Bruce added. "But I've been doing this long enough that my gut instinct tells me about people, and it tells me that she wouldn't know how to go about murdering someone. She'd be more inclined to talk someone to death than do anything physical."

"I sort of like her," Connie admitted. "More than sort of. It's as if she's telling the truth, that she knows me and we're good friends. The poor kid claims she has no place to go, that she doesn't know a soul in town except me and a couple of my friends. So"—she hesitated a moment, then blurted out—"I'm thinking of inviting her to stay at my apartment."

Bruce looked at her as if she might be as crazy as Angie Amalfi. "You're kidding me. Haven't you ever been warned about not taking your job home with you? Usually, it's meant in an emotional sense. Not physically. In this case, you'd be putting yourself in danger. That's not smart, Rogers."

"Look, she didn't have to tell me about the body in the apartment. Not about the body in the park either, come to think of it. I'm a cop. How much more dangerous can she be than what I live with every day?"

"Except that the body in the park was a victim of the

Zodiac, or a damned good copy-cat killer, which I doubt. I'm not suggesting she's the Zodiac, but we don't know that he doesn't have an accomplice."

"Nothing suggests she's any such thing."

"Still." Bruce shook his head.

"I know she's strange," Connie said. "I know none of this is rational, but I'm sure she's no killer. I'll take her home and keep an eye on her. There's something I'm missing, and I want to find out what that is. Anyway, it's the least I can do. I know I haven't been much help in this job since getting out of a patrol car and working with you."

"You're new. Who knows if this assignment will work out for you or not. But it's not worth risking your life over."

"This may be a way for me to earn my keep around here. Let me ask her."

"If you do, I'll keep an eye on you," Bruce said.

"What would Mrs. Whalen say to that?"

"Nothing good, but that's par for the course." He frowned. "We've separated. She's filing for divorce. The life of a cop and marriage don't exactly go together."

Connie heaved a weary sigh. "So I've been told."

Chapter 7

ANGIE WAS UPSET about going with Connie to her house, not because she disliked Connie, but because she would have preferred to be with Paavo. But not *this* Paavo. She missed her tough cop. Mr. Hari Krishna didn't cut it.

Still, she realized that for all the talk about the wild, free-love seventies, things were still pretty uptight. At the same time, some of what she heard made her want to warn people that herpes, HIV and Aids were on their way. Yet, she knew there was no way she could begin to explain. Even if she could, no one would believe her.

Connie drove to a Rexall drugstore for Angie to pick up a toothbrush and a few other necessities. Her car was a Ford Pinto, which Angie had never heard of, but it was cheap and used little gas. If she thought people in her time were anxious about gas, it was nothing compared to these days. Everyone believed big, gas-guzzling cars of the past were dead. She guessed they would be stunned at the popularity SUVs and Hummers would gain in a few years.

Angie had to borrow money from Connie to pay for her purchases. She had a fair amount of cash in her wallet, but she couldn't chance using the new bills. How she was supposed to get more money, she didn't know. Not only did her ATM card not have an ATM to go with it, her bank didn't seem to exist yet.

Knowing the future put everything in perspective, she realized. And made the present quite weird. She wished she could get her hands on a history book so she could better understand what was coming next. Now, however, it wouldn't be history...it would be fortune telling.

So much for that idea.

For dinner, Connie put a couple of chicken TV dinners in the oven and made a simple salad.

As they ate, they talked a bit about Angie's problem.

"You have something more going on than amnesia," Connie said between bites. "But if you won't open up to me, I have no idea how to help you."

"I don't know what's going on." Angie had an idea, but Connie would have her committed if she explained it.

"If there's something troubling you deep down, a spiritual issue in a sense, I know a man who might be able to help you," Connie said.

"A psychiatrist?" Angie asked.

"No, not at all. His name is Reverend Jones. He's wonderful. Why don't you come with me to one of his sermons at his Temple?"

"I don't think so, Connie." Angie was born and raised Roman Catholic. She might not attend church as often as she knew she should, and certainly had her less-than-saintly faults, but in her heart she believed in the tenets of the faith.

"Well, I'll tell you, it's normally not me either, but Jim has changed my mind about all that. He's quite something!"

"Jim...Jim Jones?" Angie asked, as something stirred in her brain. "You aren't talking about the People's Temple, are you?"

"I am!" Connie smiled. "There! You do remember some things."

Angie remembered all right. She had no idea when it would happen, but she knew Jim Jones would eventually move his People's Temple to Guyana, and—it was coming back to her now—a congressman from the San Francisco area would go down on some kind of "fact finding" mission, he would be murdered, and that would drive the paranoid Jones over the top. He served his followers Kool-Aid laced with cyanide, and all of them, over nine-hundred people, died.

"It's surprising," Connie said, "that anyone with such a common name could be so special, but he is. He does all he can to promote integration and has adopted children from all races. Some of the things he says are, frankly, outrageous, such as his devotion to socialism and Marxism. But he does it only for publicity, I'm sure. If he meant it, he wouldn't meet with so many top political leaders."

"He does?" Angie never heard that. She couldn't help but wonder if that side of Jim Jones was scrubbed from the history books after what was to come.

"Oh, yes! Rosalynn Carter, Jerry Brown, Walter Mondale, Willie Brown, George Moscone, Harvey Milk...the list goes on and on. They all think he's simply wonderful!"

"Holy shit!"

"That's very blasphemous in this context, Angie."

Angie put down her fork. She had no more appetite. "Connie, you've got to keep away from him!"

"What do you mean? Why?"

"Things aren't going to go well. His political supporters are going to drop him. The government will go after him. Trust me, you don't want to be involved."

Connie looked angry. "You can't know that!" She stood up and began to clear the dinner dishes.

Angie clutched Connie's arm and looked at her intently. "Promise me that when he leaves the country, you won't go with him."

"You're scaring me, Angie," Connie said, pulling her arm free.

"Good! You should be scared. Now promise me!"

"All right!" she cried, putting the chicken bones in the trash. "I promise that if he ever leaves the country, which he won't, I will not join him."

Angie shut her eyes a moment. "Thank you."

Soon after, Connie put sheets and a blanket on the sofa in the living room for Angie, and they said a chilly good-night to each other.

Angie waited until the sounds of snoring were heard from Connie's bedroom, then reached into Connie's purse and took out her car keys.

As Angie drove off in the small, weakly powered Pinto, she felt as if she were in a soap-box derby car.

She headed south on the freeway to Hillsborough where her parents lived.

She reached their street, but it wasn't a street. It was a country lane. The spot where their house should have been was a field. Then she remembered. Their house hadn't been built until 1989 or so.

Where were they?

She headed back to San Francisco, to her sister

Bianca's house. Bianca was her eldest sister, and always there for Angie, even mothering her in a way that their rather bossy mother never did.

To her surprise, when she reached Bianca's house, a Christmas tree filled the front windows and it was still brightly lit. Bianca always went to bed around eleven o'clock, and it was almost one in the morning. That alone gave Angie pause.

She went to the window and peeked in.

Then quickly backed away.

It looked like an orgy. Fortunately, Bianca wasn't included.

"Hey, ducky, I seen you peeking through the window. Why don't you come join us?"

She looked up to see a long-haired man standing in front of the door. He was stark naked except for a Santa Claus hat on his head.

Cheeks burning, she ran to the car and drove away.

At her sister Frannie's house, an old woman in a bathrobe answered the door. "Who the hell are you waking me up this time of night?!"

"I'm looking for my sis—, I mean, Frannie Levine. She lives here with her husband Seth and their little boy."

"Levine? Jewish? Humph! Sounds like some of those New York hippie types taking over this city. Well, they don't live here. And don't bother me again or I'll have you arrested." She shut the door and Angie just stared at it a moment.

She turned away from the house. Being arrested was becoming a definite theme.

Angie's third sister, Maria, was married to a man who played the horn at a jazz nightclub on Broadway. It was almost closing time, but Angie went there to see what was going on.

What should have been a jazz nightclub was a topless bar. Angie stopped at an open space in front of a fire hydrant. Should she go in? Did topless bars use live music?

Only one way to find out. She turned off the engine, locked the car, and hurried past the barker. A band played. As the topless dancer shimmied and gyrated wearing little besides a reindeer's antlers and a tail, Angie waited for the song to end. She had never seen anything like it, and gaped, goggle-eyed, at how hideous it was. When the music finally stopped, she asked the pianist if he knew Dominic Klee or Maria Amalfi Klee. He never heard of either one of them.

She would have gone to her sister Caterina Amalfi Swenson's home, but Cat lived in Tiburon, across the Golden Gate Bridge. Angie pretty much suspected what she would find if she went there. Nothing.

Traveling through time was trying, not to mention exhausting.

Maybe she should go to sleep. Maybe when she woke up, all would be back to normal again.

With that hope, she drove back to Connie's apartment.

Chapter 8

YOU SURE CAN sleep," Connie said, opening the curtains in the living room casting light on a sad little green tree on a tabletop. The ornaments and tree lights were still in boxes on the floor.

Angie looked at the clock—7:30 a.m. She hadn't returned to Connie's until nearly 2:30, and then couldn't fall asleep. Now, she was having trouble waking up. She pulled herself up a bit, propped on one elbow. "What year is it?"

"What are you talking about?" Connie asked.

Angie wasn't sure what to say. "Where's Lily?"

"Who's she?"

That was Connie's dog in Angie's world. Now, she knew she wasn't yet back in her own time. She dropped her head back on the pillow. "Just a dog I once knew."

"A dog? Sounds like a description of some of my former boyfriends. Not to mention my ex." Connie fastened the buttons on her uniform. "If you mean a real dog, now you're talking. I've always wanted a dog. But with my job's crazy hours....Anyway, speaking of my job, I've got to get going. I left some phone numbers on the coffee table for you, and there's eggnog in the fridge, and a fruit cake, if you want something to eat."

Angie didn't want food or eggnog or to call anyone in this world. All she wanted to do was to go back to sleep. She had been dreaming she was home again, and loved the feeling. She didn't want anything more to do with this alien time or place. She turned over and shut her eyes.

"I asked Paavo to come and look in on you later. Too-da-loo!"

Angie mumbled a response and was soon fast asleep.

Angie awoke to the sound of the doorbell. She opened her eyes and was immediately disoriented. *Where am I?*

She sat up on the sofa. It was Connie's apartment, but at the same time, it wasn't. What was wrong? Then it all came crashing back to her.

Her life had gone kaput.

A deep sadness, worse than she ever felt before, weighed her down. The doorbell rang once more. Her shoulders felt so heavy she didn't think she could move. Was that the third or the fourth ring? And who could it be?

Vaguely, the memory of Connie telling her she was going to work struck, and that Paavo would come over.

Paavo! Connie had put a bathrobe on a chair for Angie to use, and she wrapped herself in it now.

She was about to press the buzzer that opened the front door when caution struck. *What if it isn't him?*

The main door to the six apartments in Connie's building had a panel of thick glass with a lacy curtain in front of it. Angie ran down the stairs, went to the door and slid the curtain back a smidgen, just enough to see the landing. No one was there.

What if it had been Paavo and he gave up and left?

She hurried out to the street, but still saw no one.

Someone had been ringing the doorbell, however.

She walked, barefoot, to the next apartment building, wondering if whoever rang her bell had been a delivery man or some such thing and moved on to the next building. But still, no one.

She continued down the block when she realized that she was walking around on the street barefoot wearing an oversized bathrobe, hair uncombed, face unwashed, no makeup, and probably looking like the crazy woman others thought she might be.

She turned to go back inside when she heard music.

Now, I know I'm crazy, she thought, as she looked around.

She didn't see where it was coming from, but she distinctly heard what sounded like a saxophone playing "I'll Be Home for Christmas." She never liked that song. It always made her sad since the next line was something like "if only in my dreams." She hoped it wasn't prophetic.

She stomped back into Connie's apartment building and slammed the door.

Paavo had to admit to being nervous as he headed up the steps to Connie's apartment. Earlier, when he received no answer, he drove back to his place to get Connie's key. She had given it to him when they were dating. Boy, had that ever been a mistake! They decided they got along much better as friends than lovers, so he kept the key to her place, and she kept the key to his.

He had been shocked when Connie told him Angie Amalfi was at her house. For all they knew, she might be a murderer, somehow connected to the killing of Aloysius Starr. Why she would do that, though, made no sense to him. After all, she was the one who told him that she found Starr's body in an apartment. She claimed it was her apartment, but the woman was clearly a basket case.

Oh, well. He shrugged it off. Connie was the cop, not him, so she should be the one making sense of all this.

It was weird that Angie had thought he might be a cop. He had reacted with indignation, but he had to admit that there was much about Connie's job that fascinated him. Not that he wanted to do it. For one thing, he was opposed to guns. They should be banned. Even by cops. After all, they didn't use guns in England, and look at how much less violent crime took place in that country. He liked to envision a world with no guns, no violence, and world peace.

He often meditated on it.

Angie had finished stringing lights and had started hanging ornaments on Connie's small tree when she heard a key in the lock. The door opened.

"Connie?" she said, but instead of Connie, Paavo entered.

She froze. The need to go to him and hold him, to have him tell her everything would be fine, was a physical ache.

"Are you all right?" he asked, looking at her warily.

She immediately realized he wasn't the man for her to cling to. It hurt, and the lump that formed in her throat made it impossible to speak as she added a few more ornaments.

"Angie?"

"I'm just fine!" She whirled towards him and spat out the words. "I don't know who I am, where I live, what I'm doing here, and people that I recognize don't know me. I'm absolutely 'hunky-dory.' How's that for an old fashioned term? One you should understand."

"It's old, all right. My mother uses it."

That jarred her. She looked at him, puzzled. "You know your mother?"

His brow lifted. "Know her? How could I not? She calls and visits all the time, a real pain in the...well, anyway, thank God she lives in San Diego. She likes the weather down there better than San Francisco's."

Angie nodded. Maybe there were things about this world that were better in some ways. Her Paavo barely knew his mother and was greatly troubled by it. She turned back to the ornaments. "And your father?"

"He's with her."

No, that didn't make sense. She thrust up her chin. "How did you get such a strange name as Paavo Smith. Paavo is a Finnish name!"

"So?" He began to help her. "My mom's Finnish and named me after her father. Put it together with my father, Benjamin Smith, and you end up with Paavo Smith. I don't see what's so strange about that, except, of course, in California."

"In California?"

"You know all the people moving here from Mexico. Since *pavo* means turkey in Spanish, they find my name pretty funny. I try to ignore their laughs."

She rolled her eyes. Her Paavo would give anyone who attempted to find his name humorous "the look" and they wouldn't say a word. His blue eyes could go so hard and icy that nobody dared cross him. She hadn't called him The Great Stoneface early in their relationship for nothing.

She handed him the star that went on the top of the tree. "I can't quite reach—"

"It's okay." He put it in place.

As they both stepped back to admire their handiwork, she remember how *her* Paavo had helped her decorate the tree in her apartment. She wasn't going to bother with it this year, saying she had too many other things to do, but he thought it would be sad to miss some of the joy of Christmas and so she went along with him.

Now, she realized how much she cherished the time they had spent together.

With a sigh, she thanked this familiar looking stranger for helping her. "By the way, there's coffee," she murmured.

"Super!" Paavo went into the kitchen.

He drank a couple of cups while Angie made a cheese omelet for herself. Paavo had claimed he wasn't hungry and didn't like to eat breakfast anyway...until he smelled her omelet cooking. She gave him hers, and made herself a second. She found marmalade in the refrigerator and put it in front of Paavo for his toast.

"Far out!" he said. "I really like marmalade."

"I know," Angie replied as she finished cooking her omelet.

"Has any of your memory come back to you yet?" he asked as he ate.

"No. Nothing that makes any sense, anyway."

"And you still can't remember where you met the man in that apartment?"

She shook her head, then sat across the table from him to eat.

"It's my theory that he might have met you somewhere and took you back to his place," Paavo suggested. "There, something happened, and you killed him—in self-defense, of course—and ran out so horrified by what you did that you created an entirely different reality in its place."

She gaped at him, then took a few bites before answering. "I think I saw that movie, too, Paavo. Even if I didn't, it's a story that's been done a gazillion times."

"Well, it could be true, couldn't it?"

She dabbed her lips with a Santa Claus napkin. "It doesn't explain why I know you and Connie, does it? Or Nona, or anybody else."

"The truth is, Angie, you don't really know any of us. You simply think you do. You showed up at my house— okay, we met somewhere and I don't remember. I'm sorry. But from then on, everywhere we've gone, everyone we've seen, you've been cued to ahead of time. You decided you knew them after hearing their names. That's all."

"It runs deeper, Paavo."

He shook his head and looked at her in a way she didn't appreciate.

She stood up and put their dishes in the sink. "Look, I can take care of myself today. You don't have to miss work because of me. Go to your job. Maybe by this evening I'll be better."

"I don't mind missing work," he said.

"You don't?" She was again stunned by this new side to her fiancé.

"Not at all. I do it all the time."

"Are you sure you haven't been possessed by the spirit of Stan Bonnette?" she asked, thinking about the fellow who lived in the apartment across the hall from her—or should live there, if she lived in her apartment, which obviously she didn't because the dead Aloysius Starr lived there. God, but she hated all this!

"The spirit of Stan Bonnette," Paavo repeated, puzzled. "What does that mean?"

"Oh, sorry. I'm just raving again."

"But how do you know Stan Bonnette."

She rubbed her forehead wearily. "He's my neighbor."

"I know him as well, but not where he lives," Paavo said, standing. "Why don't we ask him, then we'll find your apartment."

"We've found my apartment already, but a corpse was in it!" How could Paavo be so dense? "Stan lives right across the hall from that apartment."

"Stan Bonnette couldn't afford a closet in that building, let alone an apartment on the top floor."

In her world, Stan's father paid for it. Why, she wondered, should this world be any different? "Still, I do know him, and since you do as well, that proves I know people you do before you mention them! It proves I'm not making this up as I go along!"

"But it doesn't. Stan's a reporter. Every so often, the *Chronicle* gives him a by-line. You probably saw it and remembered his name."

She was furious. "You're being pigheaded! Out of all the people in the world who are journalists, why would I use one whose name nobody knows!" She quickly tried to think of some well-known San Francisco journalists, and could come up with...one. "Did I say you were like Herb Caen? No! I used the name Stan Bonnette. That's because he's a personal friend. Not for any other reason."

"Why don't we go see him and find out," Paavo said.

She wasn't sure she liked the sound of that, but she was very sure she liked the idea of getting out of the apartment.

"I'll take a quick shower and be ready to go in fifteen minutes."

"I'll clean up the kitchen while you do that."

After a shower, she felt ready to face the world. Not too ready, though. She didn't have any clean clothes or her own make-up. She tried to use Connie's Max Factor foundation, but since Connie's skin tone was that of a somewhat blushing blonde, the shade was so incompatible with Angie's brunette coloring, it made Angie look like she had died. She washed it off.

She went to Connie's closet, and found a dress that had a belt she was able to pull tight enough that it didn't hang on her like a bag. She had to get her own clothes dry cleaned right away.

Time to meet a supposedly gainfully employed Stan Bonnette. This world was even stranger than she thought.

Angie and Paavo entered the *Chronicle* building and were directed to Stan Bonnette's desk. She had planned to remain completely calm and collected. He was, supposedly, a reporter after all.

Then she saw him. "Stan Bonnette!" Angie gasped. "I don't believe it!"

He turned, looked at her, and stood.

His hair was not only long, but was pulled back into a pony tail. She couldn't begin to express how ugly it looked. Also, where the Stan she knew was always immaculately dressed, this Stan wore jeans, a Grateful Dead tee-shirt, and dirty tennis shoes that had holes where the little toes should have been. A clearly misshapen corduroy jacket hung off the back of his chair. The jacket looked like it was once camel color, but now was filthy.

Stan's gaze drifted appreciatively but also curiously over Angie, as if he were trying to figure out who she was, and if he once knew her, how in the world he had forgotten.

His eyes lingered a moment on her diamond engagement ring, and from there to her Cartier wristwatch. It was a classic style with Roman numerals. She noticed that most people wore digital watches. She found it interesting that as the years went by, they grew tired of looking at 01:58:26, and found it easier to take a quick glance at a traditional watch face and think to themselves, "It's almost two."

If she fell low on funds, she might be able to pawn the watch...as long as it didn't have a date in the future anywhere on it. She would have to check.

"Have we met?" he asked.

"How else would I recognize you?" she asked right back.

"You could know me from my stories."

"That doesn't mean I'd know what you look like," she pointed out.

"Uh, yeah," he admitted. He noticed Paavo lingering in the background, not saying a word. "But I do meet everyone who's anyone in this city, so you easily might have seen me with some politicians. You want to know anything, talk to Stan the Man." He looked from her to Paavo. "That is, unless I'm interrupting something..."

"Not at all," Paavo said.

"In that case," Stan said, smiling at Angie, "are you busy Friday night?"

Angie's eyebrows rose. Arrogance obviously carried across time. "Yes, I'm busy!"

"Well, maybe some other time. Saturday night?"

She shook her head.

"She's here," Paavo interrupted, "to find out about Aloysius Starr and Alan Trimball. You're covering those murders, right?"

Stan didn't take his gaze off Angie. He looked crushed for a moment, but quickly got over it. "You knew Starr and Trimball?"

"No, I didn't," Angie said. "But I know Nona Farraday."

"And," Paavo added, "the police think Angie might have something to do with the murders. Or the Zodiac killings."

"Zodiac? I hardly think they're serious about that," Stan said with a smirk as he faced Angie again. "Since you know Nona, what's she like? Do you think she killed her chef?"

"No, I don't. Nona's a lovely person. She'd never kill anyone." The words were no sooner out of her mouth than Angie realized she had lied in exactly the same way as everyone else when asked about a crazed killer. Suddenly, it all made sense. The press came on like a bunch of bloodsuckers, and a sane person didn't want to give them anything to suck the blood of.

Nevertheless, Angie couldn't believe she had just defended Nona Farraday!

Stan studied her a moment, then asked, "What can you tell me about Alan Trimball and Nona Farraday's relationship...especially outside of work?"

"Nothing," Angie said.

"They weren't involved," Paavo added. "Nona is seeing me."

"That's not the way I hear it," Stan said.

"Nona and Alan?" Angie was aghast, but at the same time she could kick herself. What did she care if her worst enemy was two-timing her fiancé? Served him right!

"What do you know about the murders?" Stan asked.

"Nothing," Angie said. "And I have the distinct impression that you don't either."

"As I said, I'm not into the crime beat. What I like to cover is politics! I want to become the top reporter in City Hall."

Oh no, Angie thought. "Who's mayor?"

Stan glanced at Paavo. "Joe Alioto, of course. And Moscone will be inaugurated in January. Where have you been?"

She felt herself go pale. She knew what was coming to City Hall before long. She hated the thought of Stan being there when bullets started flying.

But that was silly. No reporter had been hurt in the Moscone-Milk assassinations.

Still, could she sit back and do nothing?

What if Stan's being there changed history and he got hurt or killed? "There are other things going on in the area," she said. "Why not head down to Silicon Valley? Not only will it be interesting over the years, but you'll be able to make a lot of money if you understand what it's all about."

"Silicon Valley? What's that?"

"The Santa Clara valley area close to San Jose. Buy property, start covering technology. And, while you're at it, buy Microsoft and Apple."

"Buy an apple?"

"Trust me. Stay away from City Hall."

"You're crazy."

Angie only shook her head; it was useless to argue.

"My job is in San Francisco. I can't go to Santa Clara! I cover the news right here."

"The biggest news here is to prove Nona Farraday is innocent, and you said you aren't interested," Angie pointed out.

"It's not that I'm not interested, I don't have any leads."

"I do," Angie said and was only slightly exaggerating. "How about the Individual System for Meaning Institute?"

"ISMI? The murders have to do with that?"

She didn't say yes or no, she only smiled knowingly, which was the sort of thing to capture any reporter's curiosity.

Chapter 9

AFTER THE MEETING with Stan, Angie went with Paavo to Nona's, A Restaurant so she could get started with dinner preparation. She doubted being a chef at Nona's would require dealing with many customers at one time.

Plus, with it being a macrobiotic restaurant, Angie discovered, the wholesale food costs were quite low. And if it spoiled, when you're eating little more than tofu and seaweed, who could tell?

The best thing about the restaurant was its location—Union Street near Fillmore. Angie knew the spot was going to become more and more valuable as the years went by.

Winslow Louie was already there waiting as Angie and Paavo reached the restaurant. He was a young Chinese man, thin, not much taller than Angie, with thick black hair that refused to lie flat. His job was as the dishwasher and to keep both the kitchen and dining room neat and tidy.

When Paavo unlocked the doors, Winslow went straight to the kitchen and began washing down the countertops and chopping boards since the kitchen had been closed for a couple of days.

Angie was rinsing Swiss chard and kale when she

heard a woman's voice.

"I can't believe we're supposed to work today. How can we, when Alan's dead and Nona Farraday is in jail for his murder? Doesn't anyone have a sense of decency anymore?" The woman was shaped like a pencil with a mass of curly black hair held off her face with a colorful head band. She wore no make-up.

"Who are you?" Angie asked.

"Matilda."

"That's a very pretty—"

"Finkelstein. You wanna make something of it?"

"I beg your pardon?"

"A lot of people think Finkelstein is a funny name. It shows up in comedy routines. It's nothing to joke about."

"Of course not."

Matilda's eyes turned toward Winslow with a glare. "You're actually willing to work?"

"My sense of decency," Winslow said, "begins and ends with my paycheck. No one will pay us to sit home and mourn."

"Hah!" Matilda put her bony wrists on her hard-to-find hips. "You should talk! You have no business holding a job like this anyway, not with your hot-shot Berkeley law degree. Too bad you sucked at it. Or maybe you worked here hoping Alan would hire you for that lawsuit he was always talking about! How did that work out for you? I have no sympathy for you or your paycheck!"

Winslow's ears reddened and he turned away, going back to washing a cutting board a second time.

"What lawsuit?" Angie asked Matilda.

Matilda snorted. "Who the hell knows? He was always talking about suing somebody to make it big."

With that, she went out to the dining room.

A very Irish-looking young man with reddish-brown hair and green eyes strode up to Angie. His mouth, cheeks and chin were puckered like a bulldog, and his already upturned nose, held high.

"Who are you?" Angie asked, when she didn't see Paavo nearby.

"Greg Reed. I was Alan's assistant. I was going to cook since he's dead, or are you taking his place?" His voice was so big it echoed in the kitchen.

"Well, in a sense. I'm—"

Gregory's already ruddy face grew brighter. "The murderous bitch didn't wait long to replace him, did she? I'll bet she's figuring the publicity is going to make her even more money. I can't stand it! I'm leaving."

"Wait!" Angie called. "I'm not replacing Alan. I'm just here to help Paavo for a few days. Nona Farraday is innocent. If you know her at all, you would know she isn't the type to go around poisoning anyone. And even if she was, do you think she'd have poisoned him with her own cooking? Think about it."

He pouted and shrugged.

"Anyway, Greg," Angie continued, trying to be nice, "what brings you to this job?"

"It's a job. They aren't easy to come by, in case you haven't heard. Who the hell are you to be asking me anything?"

Angie smiled as pleasantly as possible. "Just trying to be friendly."

"Well, don't!"

Angie bit her lip. She was on the verge of telling him what she thought of his rudeness, but forced herself to maintain control. She couldn't afford to offend the sous chef and have him leave.

By five o'clock, waiter Lorenzo McCaffrey arrived. Angie actually thought Lorenzo McCaffrey was a much weirder name than Matilda Finkelstein, but nobody asked, and she decided it was best to keep such observations to herself.

Matilda and Lorenzo set up the tables in the dining room, while Angie and Gregory Reed prepared the food, and Winslow Louie filled in anywhere he was needed—which was not often, as far as Angie could tell.

Paavo looked over the accounts. He seemed to think that because he was a teller, he knew something about business finances. Angie bit her tongue.

At one point, Angie noticed she was alone with Gregory. "So, what do you think happened here, Greg?" she asked as she sliced onions.

He was sautéing mushrooms in olive oil. "I don't know, but I don't think Nona killed Alan. She liked him. Besides, he did a lot of work for much lower wages than most chefs would take."

"Why was that?" The onions made her eyes water.

"Because he wasn't really a chef. He knew how to cook, but he wasn't all that great."

"So why did he do it?"

"I guess he couldn't get a better job." He added butter to the mushrooms, which wasn't kosher macrobiotic, but Angie approved.

"I guess not. Tell me about Alan," she said, wiping her eyes. "What was he like?"

"He was good-looking. Everybody noticed that about him. Even Nona. She took one look at him, and her eyes lit up. She gave him recipes, and he followed them without any changes. That's not a real chef!"

"Interesting," Angie murmured, wondering if Greg

77

Reed wasn't more of a chef than Nona recognized.

Matilda Finkelstein burst into the kitchen full of excitement when the first customers arrived.

The evening went well enough, with Matilda Finkelstein seeing every slight, every low tip, every morsel of food left on the plate as a personal insult and affront. She was constantly ready to go out and argue with the customers, and Angie had to stop her. Paavo should have been the one doing that, but whenever Matilda entered the kitchen with "that look" on her face, he cowered in a corner.

Why, Angie wondered, did Nona put up with her?

It wasn't until the restaurant closed that Angie got an answer. When she put all the tips together, Matilda refused to take her share. "I don't take tips! They're nothing but capitalistic handouts. I don't take handouts from anyone for any reason."

So Lorenzo and Winslow got her share. They sang her praises as they took the money she helped them earn, and she beamed from it.

Soon, everyone left the restaurant except Angie and Paavo. "Nona called earlier," Paavo said. "She'd like me to see her at the jail. I'll drop you off at Connie's first."

"I'd love to see Nona," Angie told him. "Maybe she'll remember me."

She helped Paavo close up the restaurant, including switching some of the money she had brought from her time with older bills in the cash register. The last thing she needed was to be arrested as a counterfeiter.

Finally, as they left, she took Nona's keys from Paavo and locked the doors. Then, talking non-stop so Paavo didn't notice, she carefully put the keys into her purse.

oOo

Nona Farraday, wearing an orange jumpsuit, faced Paavo and Angie in City Jail's interview area. She was medium height and willowy, with enormous green eyes, a heart-shaped face and flowing, shoulder-length blond hair. "I'm really unhappy about this, Paavo. This is absolutely ridiculous!" Her jaundiced gaze fell on Angie. "Is that woman with you?"

"This is Angie Amalfi," Paavo said. "She's suffering a bit of confusion, but she's a great cook and helping me at your restaurant."

"Hello, Nona," Angie said. "Don't you remember me?"

"Should I?" Nona glared at her. Angie glowered back, immediately feeling as if her whole body wanted to arch, her fingers to form claws, and a hiss to fall from her lips. Nona was clearly fighting the same urge. The air became charged with an immediate and intense dislike. At least, Angie thought, some things did not change through time.

Nona faced Paavo with narrowed eyes. "Where did you find her?"

"She seems to know all of us." Paavo sounded defensive, speaking to Nona as if Angie, *his fiancée,* wasn't even there. "I don't remember her either. Still, the poor girl has no place to go. She seems harmless enough, just a little confused. Earlier, I even watched her try to call her parents and get nowhere. Connie is helping her until she gets her memory to work right. She must be a friend or relative of someone close to us."

Nona sniffed. "I'm sure I'd remember such a person."

"Would you like me to call a bail bondsman for you?" Paavo asked. "If you tell me where to find your checkbook..."

"Are you kidding me?" Nona looked more horrified by

that thought than she was at being in jail. "No way am I going to waste my money like that! I work too hard for it. Besides, what I'm losing by not being in the restaurant, I'll gain in publicity for every day I stay in jail. Being here only proves my innocence."

"Lorenzo was saying that Alan seemed upset after you returned from your vacation," Angie said. "Did you know that?"

"Upset? I don't think so. He had a lot of questions about where I'd been. I thought he might be interested in attending."

"Attending ISMI?" Angie's eyes narrowed.

"That's right." Nona's tone was arch. "It helps you become a gentler, more caring person."

"How lovely," Angie said. If Nona was a poster girl for the program, it was in big trouble. "It certainly worked. You're surprisingly calm for someone in prison."

"Why should I care about being in prison? It's almost a vacation from my usual routine."

"What about Professor Aloysius Starr?" Angie asked. "I don't understand how the police can tie you to his death."

"They can't." Nora ran a fingertip along one eyebrow, every bit as haughtily as if she were having cocktails at the Top of the Mark. "They think because he was poisoned with the same macrobiotic food that killed poor Alan, that I must have administered it to him. They're fools. Anyone could have cooked up that dish."

Anyone in the restaurant, Angie thought. She couldn't imagine anyone else making a dish like the poisoned one— not anyone who had a palate.

"Who do you think killed Alan Trimball?" Angie asked.

"I have no idea!" Nona sounded bored by the question. "Alan was a sweetheart. Everyone loved him."

Chapter 10

THE NEXT MORNING, Angie put one of Connie's Perry Como Christmas albums on a 1960's era turntable and tried to let the background music settle her anxiety.

After a cup of warm mulled cider, she decided to phone ISMI in Mendocino. She wanted to learn was the institute was all about. The main thing she learned was that its sessions—three- and five-day retreats—were expensive.

The doorbell rang. Since Connie was at work, Angie went down the stairs before answering, and discovered Stan Bonnette at the door.

"I've got something for you," Stan said when they were back in Connie's apartment. He made himself comfortable on Connie's sofa, then handed Angie two photocopies. "The originals were given to the police." The first showed a small envelope addressed "To the Beautiful Lady Who Found Miranda Higgins."

"Who's Miranda Higgins?" Angie asked.

"That was the name of the Zodiac's last victim," Stan said. "The one found by you."

Angie's stomach did a flip-flop. The next photocopy was a piece of lined binder paper, with a strange almost child-like printing on it. But the words weren't child-like;

they were creepy.

This is the Zodiac speaking.

I am unhappy because you do not know me yet. But you will.

I lay awake at nite thinking about you.

You will be warm under my hands. You will be my Slave and wait for me in Paradice.

I will have fun inflicting the most delicious pain.

I know the cops will read this letter. I have grone angry with their snooping.

There is glory in killing cops.

They cannot figgure out who I am.

Zodiac - 17   SFPD - 0

"Oh, my God!" Angie shoved the photocopies back into Stan's hands and collapsed in the chair across from him. She knew, from history, that the Zodiac was never caught, never even identified, and that the number of his victims might not have been accurately counted. "Do you think this is real?"

"It's written in his style." Stan said, laying the papers on the coffee table next to the stack of Connie's not yet mailed out Christmas cards. "Zodiac always has a few strange spellings—maybe just to throw off the police. What's important is, it sounds as if he's someone you've met, perhaps recently."

"I've met a lot of new people recently," she said, locking her eyes on Stan's. "And frankly, most of them— this whole era—seems strange to me."

He frowned. "This whole era?"

"I don't know why I said that." She thought a moment. "But I did meet a strange fellow at Land's End before I found that woman. We talked for a while. His name is Tim Burrows, I believe. He's middle aged, probably in his fifties, with blond hair that's turning gray and worn slicked straight back from a receding hairline. He's a big man— probably 6'2" or so, and heavy, with quite a bit of a stomach on him. Let's see...he wears glasses and his eyes, I think, are gray or blue. Also, he seems a bit slow. Mentally, a little off. And he's a veteran. He talked about having served in the Air Force."

Stan shook his head. "He doesn't fit the description at all. The Zodiac is highly intelligent, possibly with a genius IQ. He does wear glasses, and he is a big fellow, with military training it's believed, but other than that, the police suspect he's in his late twenties or early thirties, probably fairly good looking, with short dark hair. He gets close to people, especially women, and then kills them."

Angie swallowed hard. "How?"

"He's shot some, stabbed some, strangled some. The police psychologist says he's a sexual sadist. That's an explanation for why, in a few cases, he attacked men as well as women—couples he's found together in lovers' lane type secluded places. Maybe out of jealousy for what he doesn't, or can't, do." He shrugged. "They say he reduces his victims to objects. The hunt for them is foreplay, and then he tortures them. Murder is the substitute for a sexual act. Violence and love are intertwined in his mind, so when he writes to you specifically, you've got to be extremely careful."

"But haven't his murders taken place in spots other than San Francisco?" she asked. "Isn't it safe here?"

"One reason he's been hard to find is he travels

throughout the area. Some victims have been found in San Francisco, but also in Vallejo, Lake Berryessa, Sacramento, Santa Rosa, other nearby places, and possibly as far away as Riverside. All in all, he's suspected of being someone who has charm, brains, acts friendly toward people, and has a winning personality."

"Are you sure about the description you gave?" she asked. "I mean, the few people who really know what he looks like are all dead, right?"

"A few have survived the attacks, so I think it's more than guesswork, although I'm not privy to police files. Seriously, Angie, if anyone you've met fits the description of the Zodiac, be sure to call me immediately. Oh…and call the police, too."

"Wait…" Angie said, trying hard to remember something important. "Weren't there some other strange murders going on around this time?"

Stan looked at her quizzically. "What do you mean?"

"Wasn't there some initiation ritual that involved killing white people? I remember hearing that everyone was afraid to go out. They stopped going to restaurants, movies, anything at all. My mother told me the joke of the time was that the only people seen out on the street at night were busloads of Japanese tourists!"

"Are you talking about the Zebra murders?" Stan asked. "How can you not remember them? The trial was just a few months ago—four men caught at the Black Self-Help Moving and Storage, convicted, sentenced to life. I covered that trial. Really interesting stuff."

"You're right. They had nothing to do with the Zodiac," Angie said, finding it hard to believe all the murders and killings and assassinations and general madness that went on in and around one small city during this time.

"Anyway, keep a look out for anyone who might be the Zodiac," Stan said, "since it seems you've crossed paths with him."

"Will do," Angie murmured. Other than the glasses, the description sounded a lot like Lorenzo McCaffrey. Or Gregory Reed. Or for that matter, Stan Bonnette.

"Thank you for warning me," she said, and quickly saw Stan out the door.

As soon as Stan left, Angie called a taxi and had it take her to Homicide where she met Connie. Angie showed her the letter from the Zodiac.

"I know," Connie said. "Stan brought it here as soon as he received it. We have the original and we're hoping to pull prints off it. So far, no luck. Don't worry. You should be safe at my place."

"I don't know." Angie was badly frightened. "What if the Zodiac sent the letter to him and then watched him, knowing he'd show it to me? He might have led the killer straight to your door!"

"Don't talk that way!" Connie said with a shudder. "I'm a cop, I'm armed. The apartment is safe."

"Except that you're rarely home," Angie muttered.

Connie bit her bottom lip, knowing Angie's words were true.

"Let's talk about something else," Angie said. "I've been thinking about Nona's situation. I think we should learn more about the people who work for her."

She didn't tell Connie that—if Stan Bonnette's description of the Zodiac was correct—one of them might be the serial killer. And maybe Alan Trimball figured it out and that's why he was killed.

Of course, that didn't explain Aloysius Starr's murder. But for Angie these days, explanations were hard to come by.

"The police are quite convinced Nona's guilty," Connie said. "They're taking the evidence to the DA to urge him to go for murder one. Premeditated. They want the death penalty."

"That's crazy. You don't even know that she knew Professor Starr!"

"But we do. He phoned the restaurant several times."

"You don't know he talked to her."

"We don't know that he didn't. She won't admit that he did. But then, it's in her self-interest not to admit it."

"You're awfully suspicious, Connie."

Connie looked at her and rolled her eyes. "I'm a cop. What else do you expect?"

"I know...but it's so not you!"

"Not me?" Connie looked at her quizzically. "Who else should it be then?"

Angie opened her mouth to answer, but then decided her explanation would only make things worse.

Chapter 11

WITH NONA'S APARTMENT, restaurant and car keys in her purse, Angie took a taxi to Nona's apartment building at the foot of Van Ness Avenue, not far from the San Francisco Maritime Museum. Since her friends all lived in the same places as they did in her world, she assumed Nona did as well. The area was a lot less upscale than it had become in her time.

Nona's car key had Volvo imprinted on it, and only one Volvo 240 was parked nearby. Angie tried it in the door and it worked.

Angie's first stop was to a hardware store on Polk Street where she had copies of Nona's keys made. She would return the originals to Paavo and hope he hadn't noticed them missing.

After that, finally with a car to get her around the city, she had several long-researched and planned stops to make. Some things were even more important than poisonings or Zodiac killers.

Earlier, in the phone book, Angie had found a Salvatore Amalfi living on Taylor Street on Russian Hill.

She dialed the number, and immediately recognized her mother's voice. Angie had pretended it was a wrong number and hung up.

Now, she knocked on that Taylor Street door, and stared a long moment when her mother opened it. "Serefina," she said finally. "Don't you know me?"

"Know you?" Serefina studied her. "I don't think so. Although, I will say, you do look familiar. You have Lucchese eyes like my sister. She's back in Italy. I talk to her on the phone, but I miss seeing her. Who are you?"

"My name is Angelina. Angelina Amalfi."

"Amalfi? Then you are related to my husband's family. *Fa bene!* Why don't you come inside? My husband will be so happy to hear about a new relative."

"Thank you." Angie drew in her breath as she walked into the flat. It smelled of Christmas—the scent of the fir tree in the living room covered with ornaments she recognized—ones her mother had used for years, of votive candles around a manger scene, and wafting in from the kitchen, the aroma of fresh baked cookies.

What if, here, she came face-to-face with herself? What would happen? She remembered hearing if you ever came face-to-face with your doppleganger one of you would die. Could that be what was going on?

She turned her attention back to Serefina. "Is your husband home?"

"He's working." She led Angie to the living room where they sat.

"Oh? What does he do?"

"We...we work at a dance studio, Arthur Murray's. Sometimes." A troubled look clouded her eyes, but then she smiled. "It's fun, but it doesn't pay well anymore. Not like the old days when everyone wanted to learn ballroom dancing. But money isn't everything."

"No, it isn't." *Sal Amalfi—a dance instructor?*

Angie could see that something was very wrong here. She hoped it was simply, as her mother said, that being a dance instructor wasn't the road to riches. In her world, her father had started out with a shoe store. He used to joke that with five daughters and a wife who loved shoes, it was cheaper to own his own store even if he never had another customer. "Has your husband ever tried selling shoes? Women's shoes?"

"Shoes?" Serefina laughed. "What does he know about women's shoes? Nothing! He did try opening a hat shop once. He wanted to sell fine men's hat wear. After all, President Truman was a haberdasher, you know. That influenced Salvatore. But he no sooner got the shop open, than President Kennedy came along and didn't even wear a hat to his inauguration! That jinxed the shop. Everybody stopped wearing them. And then the young people all started growing their hair long like the Beatles, and didn't even wear baseball caps, which was Sal's fallback. Eventually, the shop closed, and took all our savings with it. Nothing much goes on in San Francisco except the dock, and the Longshoremen. Sal is too old to do that."

"This city is going to become a great financial center," Angie said. "So do whatever it takes to buy property. Any property. And keep buying it."

"Who has money for property?" Serefina asked wryly. "Not me. I'm perfectly happy renting."

"Try," Angie urged. "It'll be worth it to you."

Serefina looked at her oddly. "You're a very strange young lady, but I do like you. Your name may be Amalfi, but you look like you're related to the Lucchese family."

"I'm sure I am."

"It's funny about your name," Serefina said, her voice wistful. "Angelina. If I ever had a daughter, I was going to name her Angelina."

"Yes, except that Salvatore never got along with your father, Angelo, so you'd have to choose other names first before you ever got around to naming a daughter after him."

Serefina's face turned white as a ghost. "How do you know that?"

"Uh..." Angie's mind went blank a long moment. "It must have been something I heard somewhere. Do you have any children?"

Serefina looked unconvinced and stared warily at Angie. "No, we were never so blessed."

The words were a stab to Angie's heart. She dropped her gaze as she asked, "Is Pa...uh, I mean, Salvatore at the dance studio now? I'd like to meet him."

"He's got a part-time job at the Emporium. In men's wear." Serefina seemed to shake off her confusion over Angie as a different sort of trouble filled her eyes. "Sal tried to teach 'disco,' which is what everyone wants to learn, but it was hard on him and, I'm sorry to say, he looked a bit ridiculous doing it. It's not dancing—just standing around and shaking."

Angie blinked back tears. "I'm so sorry."

"It's nothing for you to be sorry about!" Serefina said. "It's simply the way of the world. *Allora, dimmi, cara mia,* tell me what's wrong. You look so very sad."

"Nothing. I'm just being foolish." Angie couldn't take any more. She stood. "I should leave, but...can I give you a hug?"

Serefina also stood. "A hug? Of course." She held out her arms and Angie went to them. The scent of her mother was as she remembered it. Her tears fell over all the wonderful memories of her childhood that had no place in this world, of Christmases past with her parents and sisters and, of course, Paavo. Of Christmases that she might never have again.

"I think you miss your family very much," Serefina said. "How did you say you're related to my husband?"

"I didn't." Angie tried to wipe her tears but they kept falling. "I no longer have a family." She cried harder.

"*Poverina*. Come with me," Serefina said, pulling a handkerchief with embroidered edges from her dress pocket and handing it to Angie. "Let's go to the kitchen. I'll make you a nice cup of coffee. And I have some biscotti."

"Is it your mother's recipe, with walnuts?" Angie sat at the kitchen table.

"Of course." Serefina looked at her strangely as she put on the coffee. "How did you know?"

"I don't know," Angie said glumly, unable to think up any more lies.

"It's almost Christmas, Angelina. Do you have anyone to share it with?"

Angie was ready to cry again at the thought. She shook her head.

Serefina sat across from her and patted her hand. "Then you must come here and have dinner with Salvatore and me."

"I don't want to impose," Angie said out of politeness, hoping against hope her refusal wouldn't be accepted.

Serefina studied her. "I insist."

"Thank you," Angie said. "If I'm still here, I'll come to see you."

"*Bene!* It's difficult to be alone at Christmas. Now, the coffee almost ready. Let's have those biscotti."

oOo

Nearly an hour later, Angie left her mother and father's home, her heart filled with her mother's warmth. She hadn't wanted to leave, but forced herself.

Stopping at a phone booth outside a gas station, she checked the Yellow Pages for the Emporium. She was shocked when she saw the address.

She drove downtown, parked in the Union Square garage—fortunately, some things hadn't changed—and headed for Market Street. Before her was an enormous department store, one that looked nothing like the Nordstrom's that now occupied the space. Its massive windows were decked out for the holidays, and when she entered the store, she was astounded by the enormous, gorgeously decorated tree in its center.

She rushed to the men's department. She wondered how long it would be before the store closed for good. She should warn her father that he had to find a new job or he would be out of work again.

She found a spot to hide between some tall clothes racks, and watched the people, mostly women, milling about the men's department, where every mannequin was dressed in a different colored leisure suit.

When her father appeared, she was shocked. Her father had a bad heart, and now his color was gray—much as it had been before he had the bypass surgery that saved his life.

Did they do bypass surgeries in the seventies? And if they did, what was its success rate? Could it be anywhere as good as heart medicine and care in the twenty-first century? She wondered if Sal would get the care he needed, or if...

It hurt to see her father here like this. It hurt to see

him working at a job he so obviously hated, watching customers ignore him, shunt him aside like a sick old man who couldn't possibly know how to sell them cool clothes.

The Sal Amalfi she knew had been strong and powerful. With the success of his shoe stores, he was able to buy property, starting out with small rentals, and then buying more and more until he owned several apartment buildings in the Bay Area, including the one Angie lived in. As he aged, he developed a heart condition, but received excellent, up-to-date care.

But this Sal...this Sal...

She fled the store, tears streaming down her cheeks.

Angie drove to Nona's, A Restaurant, and parked a couple of blocks away so no one there would see Nona's car. She prepared dinner, but her heart wasn't in it. All she could think about was her family, and how much she missed them.

A fair number of people showed up to dine, to Angie's surprise. The most popular dish on the menu was clearly the curried vegetables and chickpeas served over jasmine rice, with na'an on the side.

Angie left as soon as she could without waiting for Paavo to finish the bookkeeping. She got into Nona's car and headed for Nona's apartment.

"Who are you?" asked the elderly rent-a-cop who sat at the front door.

"I'm sorry to trouble you," she said softly, trying to be friendly and polite.

"Eh?" The man appeared deaf as a post.

Angie gave him a warm smile and held out her hand to shake his. "I'm Angelina Rosaria Maria Amalfi," she said, speaking fast. She knew from experience that when she said her full name, most people went completely blank and all they heard were a string of vowels. Judging from the old man's gaping expression, her ploy had worked again. Louder, she explained. "I'm a friend of Nona Farraday's. She asked me to look after her apartment while she's away."

"A friend of Farraday's you said?"

The man was even deafer than Angie had thought. She spoke louder. "That's right. She wants me to check her apartment." She dangled Nona's keys before his eyes.

"Humph," he said. "Sounds like she's as bossy with her friends as she is with me."

"I don't mind at all," Angie hollered. "But she should have treated you a lot better."

He preened. "I think so. Just because a person's old doesn't mean I can't do my job. And you don't have to yell."

"Of course not," Angie shouted. Just then, the elevator reached the first floor, the doors opened, and she got on.

Nona's apartment was like stepping onto a movie set of an old Doris Day film. Everything was white or pink and frilly. How could Nona live this way? She was the most unfrilly woman Angie had ever met. Everything about her was hard-angled and pristine, or so Angie had thought.

As Angie walked around the comfortable apartment, she couldn't help but think that Nona was locked up in jail and no one was using it tonight. For all she knew, Nona would be released the next day, but tonight...

Angie was tired of sleeping on couches, showering in a place where the water turned cold after two minutes, and wearing Connie's crummy hand-me-downs.

She felt awkward at Connie's, and while she would normally have loved to live with Paavo, staying with *this* Paavo would have felt like cheating.

A thought struck. Was she going to spend the rest of her life traveling through time? A gourmet cook version of *Doctor Who*? If so, she wished she had a Tardis. Or a magic carpet. Anything to take her back to her own time. But this wasn't really time travel. If it was, her friends wouldn't be here—they wouldn't have been born yet! And her parents would be young again. So this must be some kind of alternate reality. A forty-years-behind-the-times parallel universe.

Who was she kidding? This was a nightmare, a very real nightmare, but a nightmare. Pure and simple!

She looked in Nona's closet. Nona was taller than Angie—most people were. Actually, she looked like a fashion model, which Angie hated, since she would never be tall or svelte enough to be one, no matter what time period she was in. Not that she was heavy. Other than wishing she was a little more busty, she simply had curves where they should be.

All of which meant that Nona's dresses, which must have been embarrassingly short on Nona, managed to fit well enough.

Angie could scarcely believe it when she put on a pair of Nona's bell bottoms. Bell bottoms had made a brief comeback in Angie's time, but were worn mostly by teenagers, and weren't half as wide as these pants. These looked like something used to sail a ship.

She tried on beaded tops, a tie-dye tee-shirt, and an outfit with a floor-length peasant skirt, a crocheted top, and a long chiffon scarf that she tied around her head like a fortune teller. She laughed for the first time in what felt like a month. The colors were loud and garish, and as she twisted and turned in front of the mirror, watching the skirt swish from side to side, she thought the women of this time were pretty lucky—they could dress up in costumes whenever they wished. None of the clothes of her time were nearly so much fun.

When she opened up the lingerie drawer, however, she faced a different kind of shock. Most items were designer wear, matching, expensive Schiaparelli and a few other brands that sounded somewhat familiar. Near the bottom of the drawer she pulled out several pairs of red and black laced panties, bras, and garter belts from Frederick's of Hollywood. Amazing!

She stuffed those back in the drawer. She shuddered at the thought of Nona wearing any of that stuff. What was the woman thinking? And even worse, was she thinking it about Paavo?

Angie went into the bathroom and looked longingly at the tub. She wandered back to the living room, but kept feeling herself drawn to the bathtub like a moth to a flame. She could use a little luxury, and Nona kept a huge supply of bath salts, gels and perfumes. Why not go for it? She deserved a nice bath after all she had been through.

She phoned Connie and left a message on her answering machine that she found somewhere else to stay that night, then ran the water. In no time she was soaking in the tub, bubbles all around her. She slid down so that the water was over her shoulders, then leaned back, her head against the rim of the bathtub.

Ah, heaven!

Now, relaxing, she had time to ponder. Why she was here? Not here in Nona's apartment, but *here,* now? Was she supposed to prove something? If so, what?

What if it was to prove that Nona was innocent?

No one seemed to care that Nona was sitting in jail and hadn't killed anyone. No one seemed to recognize that but Angie. What was wrong with these people? Is that what her role was? To prove that the one person she would gladly see rot in a jail did not deserve to be there?

Was this some sort of cosmic joke?

Crazy as it was, she knew if she didn't try to free Nona she couldn't live with herself. Nona was innocent, and shouldn't be in jail.

If no one else took up the case, Angie would.

Maybe that would be her ticket home.

Her eyes grew tired and she was just about to shut them when she heard a noise.

She became immediately alert, and never felt more vulnerable. Words from the horrible Zodiac letter sprang to mind.

Suddenly, the lights went out.

Scarcely breathing, Angie stayed stark still, wondering where she should go, what she should do, when she heard music from a long distance away.

Someone was playing "Sea of Love" on a saxophone. *Come with me, to the sea...*

Angie stayed absolutely still, listening for footsteps coming closer.

But then she realized that was stupid. If someone did come in, what would she do? Rub soap in his eyes?

She quietly climbed out of the bathtub, and felt around the unfamiliar room for the bathrobe hanging from a hook on the door. She put it on, then groped in the drawers of Nona's vanity for something to use as a weapon to protect herself.

Fortunately, Nona owned one of the largest hair dryers Angie had ever seen (or, in this case, felt). She imagined Nona's arm must have ached holding it to dry her hair. Angie continued to search, and was glad she was being very careful when she found a women's razor, but its blade would make any self-respecting crook laugh. Other than hair spray, which she could try to aim into his eyes, she couldn't find anything else.

Finally, Angie tiptoed from the bathroom and went through the apartment.

She didn't see, hear or sense anyone else inside.

The saxophone continued to play "Sea of Love." She couldn't tell where the sound came from.

What was with all the saxophone players around her suddenly?

Was she being plagued by John Coltrane wannabes?

She wasn't even all that sure who John Coltrane was, but she had heard the name too many times to forget it.

Thankfully, the lights came back on, and Angie felt very foolish standing there with her "weapons" in hand due to nothing more sinister than a power glitch...or so she tried to convince herself. Pacific Gas and Electric was forever having blackouts, brownouts, and generally miserable power in her time, so why would it have been any better in the 1970's? If anything, it was probably worse!

She made sure the apartment was locked up tight, and went to bed with the hair spray, dryer, and a big kitchen knife at her side under the covers.

Chapter 12

THE NEXT MORNING, Angie drove Nona's Volvo to the Russian Hill apartment building where she lived in "her world." It had no doorman in the twenty-first century, so for sure, it had none now, even though one apartment was cordoned off as a crime scene.

Earlier, she called *The Chronicle* and learned Stan wasn't at work that day. Since she didn't know his home phone number, and the *Chronicle* wouldn't give it to her, she did the next best thing. She knocked on Stan's apartment door. She wanted to talk more about his neighbor, Aloysius Starr—the mystery man in all this.

The door opened, but it wasn't Stan who stared at her, it was a short, older man wearing a yellow shirt, brown polyester slacks, and a thick brown curly-haired toupee. Earl White!

Angie could have fallen over in a dead faint.

"Earl! What in the world are you doing here? Where's Stan?"

Earl looked confused. "Where's whozit?"

"Stan Bonnette. This is his apartment, isn't it?"

"Hell no. Dis is me and my friends place. Who're you,

lady? An' how do you know my name's Oil? 'Ey, Vinnie, dis here broad t'inks we don't belong here!"

"Who's she?"

Earl pulled the door open wider. A short, stocky, sixty-something year old with a stogie in his mouth and basset hound bags under his eyes stared at her.

"Vinnie Freiman," Angie said walking into the apartment. "Calm down, you don't want to get your blood pressure up any higher than it is."

Vinnie looked at Earl. "How the hell she know about my blood pressure?"

Earl shrugged. "How da hell she know your name?"

Vinnie stoked his chin. "True. So, lady, what'dya want?"

"I want to know about the man next door. The dead man in my apartment."

"In who's apartment? I t'ought he was in his own place," Earl said.

"Does Butch live here too?" Angie asked.

"Vinnie," Earl whispered, "she knows Butch, too."

"Scary, ain't it?" Vinnie admitted. "Who the hell is she?"

"Damned if I know," Earl admitted.

"How'd you know us?" Vinnie asked.

Angie was afraid to say. In her world these guys were petty thieves who had served time and now ran a restaurant, Wings of an Angel, as in the old song, *"If I had the wings of an angel, o 'er these prison walls I would fly..."* The three hadn't wanted to become restaurateurs, but the establishment happened to be next door to a jewelry store...and its vault....

But that was another story.

Angie managed to break up the heist and became good

friends with the three men. The very limited menu that their cook, Butch Pagozzi, served was actually quite delicious. Butch had cooked when he was in the army as well as in stir, so he knew all about cooking in quantity, and for people you didn't want to make angry by serving food they didn't like.

Angie pretended to be indignant. "I can't believe you don't remember me, but it really doesn't matter—"

"Was she one of yours?" Vinnie asked Earl.

"No way. But she might be one a Butch's."

Vinnie looked her up and down. "You ever have trouble with your feet?"

"I beg your pardon!"

"We're noises," Earl said.

"Noises?" Angie frowned with confusion. "What kind of noise do you make?"

"We don't make noise, we *are* noises. We woik down at St. Francis Hospital. Butch woiks wit' patients who have problems wit' deir feet—like a physical t'erapy type noise. Me an' Vinnie do general noising. We learned in da army."

Vinnie drew himself up as tall as his short, elderly body could go, then proudly jabbed his thumb against his chest as he added, "Not all nurses are women, you know. Our guy patients are glad to see us come in."

Angie pressed her hand to her cheek. "You expect me to believe that you three are nurses?"

"Why not? You think just because I'm short I can't be a nurse?" Vinnie shouted. "I think she's bein' mean to us, Earl."

"Dat's discrimination!"

Angie needed to take control of this madness. "What do you know about the apartment next door? Do you remember when I lived in it?"

"You? No way, lady," Vinnie said. "That's been Professor Starr's place for years."

"He woiked in Boikley," Earl added. "At da university."

"Do you have any idea who would have wanted him dead?"

"Hell no," Vinnie said. "He was a nice guy. Still had a lot of life left in him, matter of fact. He was planning to go to some class or retreat or something in Mendocino."

"ISMI?" Angie asked.

"Is you what?" Vinnie asked.

"Forget it. All I can say is Starr's death wasn't an accident."

"He was moidered?" Earl gasped.

"Do you know who's gone to visit him lately," Angie asked. "Or maybe people he knew, places he went?"

"I never saw nobody. Whadabout you, Earl?"

"I didn't see nobody neit'er. Oh...but he did like to go to Nona's restaurant."

"Oh? Do you think he knew Alan Trimball?"

"Who?"

"Keep thinking about it. I'll be back," Angie said.

Earl looked at Vinnie. "I'm t'inking we should get outta here. What if da moiderer t'inks we saw him?"

"Or," Vinnie said, nodding his head toward Angie, "her."

Chapter 13

ANGIE HEADED ACROSS the Bay Bridge to the University of California in Berkeley. What was really strange here, perhaps the strangest thing of all she'd experienced so far, was that the people in Berkeley looked exactly the same as they did in her time, with long hair that was either stringy or bushy, headbands, sandals, jeans and flowing tops. She used to feel she was stepping back in time whenever she went there, and now she knew her feeling had been right.

She entered Sproul Plaza. The Student Union building stood on one side, the administration building on the other, and in between were tables of groups pushing their agendas. CORE, SNCC, SDS, and lots of other initials she had never heard of were represented.

She located the Sociology department office, and there, she flashed her wallet with hand-written "Press Pass." She had learned from Paavo (the real Paavo) that few people read the badges and I.D.s waved at them. He'd been right. She quickly put it away and told the two female clerks she was there to write the obituary of Professor Aloysius Starr for the *San Francisco Chronicle*.

They both talked about what a wonderful man he was.

Angie had yet to meet a dead man who wasn't. It was amazing what saints the dead were. Too bad the living were all such sinners.

She then leaned on the counter and said in a stage whisper, "Don't spread this, but the police aren't telling the public everything."

The two women were all ears.

"One of Starr's students, Alan Trimball, was killed the same day as him. The police think the deaths are connected, perhaps going back to the time Alan was in Starr's class. I'd like to know who else was in that class. Maybe they can tell me something."

"We can't tell you," the blond clerk said. "There are privacy concerns."

"Starr is dead," Angie stressed. "He has no right to privacy. It's not as if he can sue you. And all I want to do is see if any of his students has any inkling of who might have killed him. You don't want to obstruct justice, do you?"

Fortunately, both women were so shaken by the possibility of Starr being murdered, they didn't think about the incongruity of what Angie was saying.

The brunette pulled a file and handed it to Angie as if it were a hot potato. "This lists Professor Starr's classes and the students in them. It should help you."

Angie zeroed in on the class that included Alan Trimball and returned the other papers. "Do you have a photocopy machine?" Angie was pretty sure they had photocopiers back then.

"Right there." Barbara pointed to a behemoth. Angie needed help to work it, and then the machine was achingly slow and loud.

As she headed to the Student Union where she hoped to find a pay phone, she saw Boalt Hall, the law school, in the distance. Matilda had said Winslow Louie had a "hotshot Berkeley law degree." Could that be what she meant?

Angie stopped at the law school office and asked about Winslow Louie. She found out he was in law school at the same time as Alan Trimball was an undergraduate. She didn't know if that meant anything or not.

Back at the main administration building, she looked up phone numbers for each student on her list. It was amazing the information freely given back then. She then went to a bank and got rolls of quarters which she took to a payphone.

Dropping coins into a box and using a rotary dial was an entirely new experience for her. They still had payphones in "her time," but she had never used one.

The money she was throwing into the phone was being wasted, she realized, as she got one "Starr was a wonderful man" after the other...until the ninth call.

A student named Cara O'Donnell said, "It's strange that he should have died at the same time as Alan Trimball."

"Why is that strange?" was Angie's obvious question.

"Because the two men had become friends."

"Really? How do you know?"

"I dated Alan for a while. He was a senior when I was a junior. I really liked him, but things didn't work out. It's always the good ones who get away, although I understand he didn't do so well after he left school. He majored in sociology, and what do you do with a degree like that? He needed to continue to get a Ph.D., or find a job in one of the great liberal education fall backs—a bank, insurance company, or the government. I didn't know where he ended up until I saw his name in the paper. A cook? That was pretty much of a comedown, I'd say."

Angie ruffled. "There are many well-known cooks. It can be a lucrative, well-respected profession."

"Oh? Name one."

It was on the tip of her tongue to name several—Emeril Lagasse, Paul Prudhomme, Wolfgang Puck, even the one who almost hired her, Poulon-Lelieullul—but then she realized that the girl wouldn't know any of them. Finally, desperately, she said, "Julia Child."

"She writes cookbooks and has a TV show. Alan was hardly in that class. He could sling hash. How he got a job in a decent restaurant, I have no idea. He probably was willing to accept dirt cheap wages and do everything the owner said without question."

That sounded like Nona Farraday's restaurant to Angie. "Do you remember the names of anyone else who was in the class with Alan?"

"No, not really, but I met him through a sorority sister, Mary Pomporino, who knew him for years. She's married now. Mary Jacobson. Let me find her phone number for you. Hold on. My address book is in my purse."

An address book—how quaint, Angie thought. All her friends stored phone numbers in their cell phones.

As soon as she was given it, Angie called the number for Mary Jacobson. The moment the woman said "Hello," Angie knew she had to see her.

Angie nervously stood at the front entry of the small Sunset district house and rang Mary Jacobson's doorbell.

In a moment, Mary opened the door, and Angie looked into the eyes of her third oldest sister. "Maria?"

The woman looked surprised. "Nobody calls me that except family. You must be Miss Amalfi. Won't you come in?"

As she led Angie into her home, she asked, "Have we met before? You look familiar."

Angie wasn't sure what to do say. "I don't think so, but I'll admit that when I saw you, something told me your name was Maria. Odd, isn't it? Do you have any sisters or brothers?"

"I don't. I was an only child."

Angie's disappointment was keen. "Well, that's not it, then."

They sat in the living room and Mary offered some coffee and cookies, which Angie took. They were almond horns, covered with powdered sugar, just like the real Maria liked to make. Tears came to Angie's eyes when she bit into a cookie and it brought back memories of her home and family. Shades of *Remembrance of Things Past* and the *petites madeleines* scene filled her. She had never understood it as well as she did at this moment.

"Are you all right?" Mary asked.

"Yes, fine." Angie put the half eaten cookie on her saucer. "Your cookie tastes just like one my sister makes."

"It's a family favorite."

Angie nodded, then got down to business. "I wanted to ask about Alan Trimball. He was recently found murdered. A friend of mine is suspected by the police, but I know she's innocent. I'm trying to find out something about Trimball. The police, frankly, don't give me any confidence."

"I know what you mean," Mary said. "But I have no

idea why anyone would want to harm Alan."

"One of his sociology professors was also found dead. Aloysius Starr. I understand Alan was a sociology major."

"What are you implying?" Mary asked.

"I'm implying exactly what you're thinking. That this might not be a coincidence, and that someone needs to look into what went on—what connected the two men."

"And you're that person?" Mary was clearly skeptical.

Angie didn't blame her. "Until someone else comes along. Why not?"

Mary shook her head. "All I can tell you is that his best friend might know something. Ask Lorenzo McCaffrey."

"They were best friends in college?"

"Yes. Quite close. We all had the same major and were in Professor Starr's class together. I remember Alan complaining about all the work and huge projects Starr gave us."

"But Lorenzo wasn't listed in the class."

"He dropped out. He couldn't keep up with the assignments. Why? Do you know Lorenzo?"

"I've met him. I had no idea..." In fact, she remembered Lorenzo specifically telling her he didn't know who Aloysius Starr was. Why did he do that? "Can you tell me anything about Lorenzo and Alan? What kind of relationship did they have?"

Maria thought a moment. "Well, for a while, the two had big plans about how they were going to get people to live in peace and harmony. Typical Berkeley stuff. Unfortunately, the plans they developed had a deep whiff of communes, which were already losing favor."

"Communes? Like in the old Soviet Union?"

"I'm talking hippie communes."

"Oh?"

"Good God, where have you been, girl? They're all over the place. Go up to Mendocino if you don't believe me."

"Oh, *those* hippie communes." Angie hoped Mary believed her. "Sure. I get you."

"Hmm. Anyway, you can see the problem. Most of their ideas were old and tired, and some were completely far out. Nothing came of them, so that was why they took Starr's class. Starr had the reputation for teaching students to stretch their minds, to come up with better, more innovative ideas than they ever could have imagined on their own."

"Did it work?"

"For Alan, it should have. He developed an idea in Starr's class that excited him. He never did anything with it, however."

"Why not?

She shrugged. "It probably took more money than he could get his hands on."

"What about Lorenzo?"

Maria shook her head. "When he dropped Starr's class, he lost his student deferment and was drafted. He was really bitter. I think he blamed Starr. For him, I guess, that was the end of any big ideas."

Chapter 14

ANGIE STOPPED IN Homicide after talking to Maria—or should she say Mary?—and gave Connie the list of students in Professor Starr's sociology class, telling her exactly how she'd gotten the lists—and why—when Connie questioned her. "Alan Trimball and Lorenzo McCaffrey were both in that class," Angie said, offering information she knew the police didn't have and probably never would have gotten without her. "I know it has something to do with the murders of Trimball and Professor Starr. It has to."

"Or it's a coincidence," Connie said.

"I talked to most of those students and some are suspicious. They say something went on in that class. They don't know what. Some said Trimball and Starr were friends. Others said they could cut the tension between them with a knife. I'm sure someone knows what happened. I've tried to get McCaffrey to talk about it, but so far he just clams up."

"Okay," Connie said. "What would you like me to do?"

"I've been able to track down all but three of the students. Janet Gray, Adam Halpernin, and Peter Lemon.

If you can find them, maybe they know something. All I can think is, it might be worth a try."

Connie sighed. "All right. I'll see what I can find out."

Angie dashed over to Nona's, A Restaurant to prepare meals for customers, if any. Also, she looked forward to talking to Paavo. She wanted to fill him in on what she had learned about the people who worked there.

But Paavo called to say he would be late since he was going to visit Nona that evening. She was feeling lonely.

Nona was in jail...what did she expect?

Angie was lonely, too!

Without Paavo there to distract her, after the last customers were served, Angie turned all her attention on Lorenzo McCaffrey.

"So Lorenzo," she began. "How did you end up working in the same restaurant as Alan?"

"A stroke of luck," he said. "I was in a bar, a topless joint, down on Broadway, and in walked Alan with a couple of guys. He started talking about this restaurant where he was a cook, and how the waiters and waitresses were making as much money as he was from tips. He said it had a really classy clientele. I said I should have a job like that, and told me there was an opening. I think he was daring me to take it. Like, I would think it was below my dignity to be a waiter when I could be laying linoleum in office buildings like I was doing. Besides, the glue gave me a headache every day, and the rolls of linoleum were damned heavy. My back was already starting to give out, so I thought, why not give restaurant work a try?"

"Smart idea," Angie said.

Greg Reed, the assistant chef, snorted.

Lorenzo ignored him. "I thought so. Then I met Nona. We hit it off." He tugged at his jacket to smooth it and stood a bit straighter. "Too bad for her she had a rule that she didn't date 'the hired help,' but it was pretty clear she liked what she saw. She might even have been thinking about changing her rule, you know. But then, she's a woman who's also pretty stuck on herself, if you know what I mean."

"I know." Angie nodded.

"I took the job. Alan was right about it. Some nights I make a killing; other nights, not so much. I meet interesting people, though. Some are nice; most I wouldn't give a pot to piss in."

"But overall, you enjoy working here?"

Winslow Louie, the over-educated dishwasher, strolled into the kitchen and stood in the doorway listening to the conversation. He had a pitcher of ice water in one hand, and a damp cloth to wipe down the dining room tables in the other. "Working? Lorenzo?" he said, a sneer on his face. "I do everything for his customers but take their order and serve the main dish!" He put down the pitcher and went to the sink to wash off the cloth.

Lorenzo fumed as he glared at Winslow, then faced Angie again. "Like I said, it's better than laying linoleum. It's a job. I got other things to think about."

"Such as?"

"Such as none of your business." He glanced at Greg and Winslow, then lifted his chin. "What's this, the Inquisition? You sound like the cops, wondering where I was and what I was doing. Well, I got an alibi for the night Alan was killed—a hundred-person alibi—so you can stop asking questions about it."

"Calm down, Lorenzo. I'm just trying to get to know

you better! You know I'm no cop!"

"Want to know me better, huh?" He gave her a quick head-to-toe perusal. "Well, there are ways to do that."

"What do you like to do for fun?" she quickly asked, not liking the way he was smirking.

His smirk grew broader. "All kinds of stuff."

Greg snickered loudly as he put left-over carrots in the refrigerator.

"What are you good at?" Angie asked Lorenzo.

"I like to party. Want to join me sometime?"

Winslow rolled his eyes and then stomped back into the dining room, clean cloth in hand.

At that moment, Paavo walked into the kitchen and greeted everyone, oblivious to the odd tension in the room. He immediately turned his attention to the night's receipts.

Angie glanced at Lorenzo. "I'd better get back to work."

Matilda came into the kitchen. She had been covering the cash register and phone. "What's going on with Winslow?"

Everyone ignored her.

Lorenzo looked at the clock. "Yeah, well, I'd like to continue this fascinating conversation with all of you, but my shift is over. I'm out of here."

Angie wondered if, now that Paavo was here, she shouldn't leave as well to see where Lorenzo was going. She was suspicious of him and wanted to know what the man was up to.

"Time for *Bullitt* in reverse," Matilda muttered, arms folded, and eying Lorenzo as if he was God's gift to women. He didn't notice.

"You said it, babe." He shrugged on his leather jacket.

"What do you mean?" Angie asked. "What bullet?"

"The movie," Matilda said. At Angie's confused look, she added, "Steve McQueen. It's a few years old, sure, but everybody knows it."

"Oh, that *Bullitt*." She had heard of it slightly.

"It's got the coolest car chase you've ever seen," Paavo said, approaching the others. "Right there on Fillmore Street. The cars zoom down it so fast, they go sky born! It's far out!"

"A car chase?" Angie asked. "Sounds lame."

"Lame?" Paavo and Matilda glanced at each other.

Angie guessed she chose an expression from the wrong era yet again. Maybe she needed to simply stop trying to come up with slang since everything she said was either too new or too old.

As she watched Lorenzo walk out the door without a backwards glance, she decided to leave as well. She said quick good-byes and rushed out, ignoring the fish-eye Matilda gave her.

Lorenzo turned up Fillmore Street. Angie ran down the block to Nona's car and caught up to him, then pulled into a driveway to wait and watch. She did it a couple more times. He didn't strike her as a person who paid any attention to cars going by, and he didn't. She wondered if he didn't have a car. She also understood what they were saying about *Bullitt*. She suspected mountain goats would refuse to walk these hills.

Three blocks later, Lorenzo turned into an apartment building. She wondered if he lived there and possibly had retired for the night. She didn't have long to wonder.

Lorenzo soon came out wearing a light overcoat. He got into an old Chevy sedan.

She followed him to Mission Street where he parked near a place called Dance A-Go-Go.

The Mission was an area Angie never went to alone in her own time, and she saw that the area was no better during this time. If anything, worse.

As Angie headed back to Nona's apartment, she realized if she wanted to know more about Lorenzo McCaffrey, it looked like she would have to learn to disco.

Chapter 15

EVEN IN NONA'S comfortable apartment and bed, Angie couldn't fall asleep that night. Instead, she tossed and turned, puzzled and unhappy. What was she doing here? Why was everything so crazy and how, in God's name, was she supposed to find her way home again?

The next morning, she drove back to Land's End. She had found a dead body there; it should have been the last place she ever wanted to set foot in again. Yet, something about it drew her—possibly because it was the only place where she felt connected to the world she knew. And the feeling, so strong she could taste it, told her that if she could ever return to her own time, it would be from here.

She heard a saxophone playing, and smiled.

Her poor, damaged friend Tim. At least he could make beautiful music.

He was slowly, emotionally playing "Stranger on the Shore." That was how she felt. It made her eyes misty.

"What's the matter?" Tim asked, putting down his saxophone when the song ended.

"Don't stop. I enjoy listening. You play beautifully."

"Thank you. I try to make people happy with my music, but that doesn't happen anymore. They used to be happy, but not now."

She thought about Dance A-Go-Go. "Maybe you need to play disco. That sounds like happy music."

"No. That's music to use to hide disillusionment."

To hear Tim say that surprised her, but she had the feeling he was right. She thought this was supposed to be a happy time, all about sex, drugs, and rock 'n' roll...or disco. Yet she sensed a bizarre freneticness to the time, as if people knew they were on the edge of something and were rushing and pushing and running, but they didn't know where to, or what from.

She knew what was coming, however. Some things were wonderful, but others so horrible it would defy these people's imaginations.

But Tim couldn't know about the future.

"Why do you say that about disillusionment?" she asked.

He shrugged, and looked blankly at her. "It's all relative."

She smiled. "So they say."

Tim's blank look, however, reminded her of what happened when people were directionless, with nothing useful or important in their lives. It was emptiness, and that was what she saw around her.

"Man does not live by disco alone," she said.

"No, he doesn't."

Tim picked up his sax and played the Etta James favorite, "At Last," as she walked away. He broke off briefly to call out, "Have a nice day!"

As if!

oOo

"You, me and Paavo need to go to Dance A-Go-Go," Angie said to Connie as she sat across her desk in Homicide. "It'll be the best way we can find out about Lorenzo."

"Lorenzo doesn't have anything to do with this," Connie said. "Everyone in Homicide thinks Nona did it. Although some of that might change if she were a little more cooperative and not so snotty to people trying to help her."

"If she's innocent and you're the one to prove it, you'll cement your career in Homicide." Angie went on to explain that Lorenzo knew both Alan and Professor Starr, and could easily have cooked up the poisonous concoction that killed them.

From what Angie had learned about Lorenzo, he was clearly jealous of Alan who was able to stay at the University and hated Starr for having such a difficult class that Lorenzo had to drop out. And Angie took it as her duty to prove his guilt and help secure Nona's freedom.

Connie shook her head. "That may be true, but it's a far cry from talking about Lorenzo's feelings to accusing him of murder!"

"That's why we've got to get closer to Lorenzo. The way to do that is through Dance A-Go-Go, where we'll be able to talk to him away from the restaurant. Catch him off guard! The only problem is, I've got nothing to wear, and no money to buy anything halfway decent."

"At least that's a problem I can help with," Connie said. "Let's go to a thrift shop I know. You'll love their clothes."

"A thrift shop?" Angie had never shopped in one before...but then, she always had money before.

"The disco outfits you find there are practically new.

Heaven forbid someone be seen wearing the same outfit twice."

"What if someone recognizes that I'm wearing her dress?" Angie asked.

"It's not as if these are exclusives. No one will know. Let's go take a look. Beggars can't be choosers."

Beggars...that's what Angie was, all right. She was glad she had convinced Paavo to pay her for the work she was doing at Nona's. She needed money. What if she couldn't get back to her own life? What if she was stuck here with these strange facsimiles of her friends? What then? She couldn't mooch off them forever. She had to find a way to live. She, who had always tried to find work doing something she loved and being maddeningly unsuccessful at it, now needed to take any job she could find, and do it well enough to keep it, simply to live. Talk about an alternate universe!

As they drove in Connie's car to the thrift shop, Angie asked Connie if she had located the three sociology students from Starr's class. Connie found that one of them had died in Vietnam, another had married and was living in Connecticut. Connie had called her, but the woman scarcely remembered being in the class let alone anything about it. The third, Peter Lemon, seemed to have disappeared off the face of the earth two years after graduating from the University. No record for him could be found anywhere. Nothing was being posted to his social security record, and no driver's license or anything else could be found.

Soon after they arrived at the thrift shop, Angie found shimmery white sateen hot pants and a matching, midriff-baring and extra-tight top that scooped low in the front and had long sleeves that flared out from the elbow. She also discovered a pair of white vinyl knee high boots with three-inch high chunky heels in her size. They looked fairly cute with the hot pants, Angie had to admit.

"I didn't realize how short hot-pants were, I mean, are," she said tugging at the material as she looked at herself in a mirror. The hot pants and top were nine dollars, the shoes two, which seemed beyond belief.

Connie grinned. "Finally, you look as if you belong."

"That would be more of a miracle than you could possibly imagine," Angie muttered.

Connie bought what she called a catsuit, a one-piece bodysuit made out of lime green spandex, with a halter top and floor-length pants that flared from the knee. Her outfit wasn't nearly as revealing as Angie's, but then Connie was a cop. The only problem was that she had no place at all to hide a gun, should they need one.

Chapter 16

PAAVO CLOSED DOWN Nona's, A Restaurant early that night so he and Angie would have plenty of time to get ready for their disco date. He used the excuse of not enough customers although, amazingly, they had more than normal.

An hour later, Angie and Paavo entered Disco A-Go-Go. Angie had left the Volvo at Nona's, knowing Paavo would be driving. Connie was supposed to go with them, but at the last minute, she told Angie she had to do a little more work at Homicide. Angie decided Connie chickened out at the thought of disco dancing. She also didn't see Lorenzo in the crowd.

"Dance with me, Paavo," Angie said, as ABBA's "Mamma Mia" began to play through every loudspeaker.

"I don't dance," he mumbled glumly.

"But..." She'd seen him. When they first met, he went undercover to a wedding to keep an eye on her since someone was trying to kill her. When he asked her to dance, she was certain the big, tough detective didn't know how and refused. He turned around and glided her mother across the dance floor, then several of her sisters before she relented. She had been dancing with him ever since. But, she realized, he didn't know that.

She sighed, and continued to search the crowd for Lorenzo, which the flash of strobe lights and the glitter from the gaudy disco ball made difficult. Maybe this wasn't such a good idea. Maybe they should just leave.

"Hello." She looked up and saw Lorenzo approach. He wore a light blue suit made of shiny, clingy polyester. It came with a vest, and its trousers flared out from the knee. With it, he had on shiny black platform shoes, and a colorful blue and yellow shirt, open at the neck with its collar flopping over the jacket.

"Join us?" she asked.

He sat.

"Do you like disco?" Angie asked, pretending she hadn't followed him there or knew anything else about him.

"Love it. Especially tonight since there's a contest."

"Did Alan like to come here, too? I've heard you two hung out together outside of work."

"No, this wasn't his scene."

"What was his scene?"

"The only thing he ever thought about was ISMI. After all, he came up with the basis for it in Starr's class. Uh, oh! The contest is starting." Lorenzo stood up and started looking around.

"Wait! ISMI was Alan's idea? What do you mean?"

"Uh...nothing. I've got to find a partner. See you!"

Angie grabbed his arm. "I can dance."

His eyes went from her head to toe a couple of times. "I'm very good at this," he said.

She wanted to learn more about Alan and hated to lose

Lorenzo to some other dance partner. "I'm a good dancer, too," she said. "I even studied ballet." She had, in fact, from ages six to ten when the ballet teacher told Serefina that even though Angie was small enough to be a ballerina, she wasn't coordinated enough. So much for dreams of being the next Margot Fonteyn.

She walked out to the dance floor and the band began a vaguely familiar tune, "That's the Way I Like It."

Lorenzo took her hand. "Just follow me," he whispered. "It'll take a while before they start to watch us, as other couples get eliminated. Then, we'll really let them see what we can do, okay?"

"Sure," she said.

She remembered seeing a contest like this in an old John Travolta movie she had once watched with her mother. To her, John Travolta was a chubby middle-aged man who played tough guy films. She was surprised to see him play a young, thin dancer. Her mother assured her that both Travolta and the film—*Saturday Night Fever*—she thought it was called, had been very popular when Serefina was a young woman.

Lorenzo took her hand, and they did some fancy side-by-side steps that she found easy to follow. She had to dance with her sisters when she was a kid. Since she was the youngest, the older girls always took the lead, and she was forced to follow them—and do it well—or they would twist her ear. She learned to be a very good follower.

She quickly caught on to the disco dance step simply by watching Lorenzo and the other dancers around her and trying to remember the movie.

He wrapped her arms around her body so that when he pulled on her hand, she uncurled in a fast spin. "Very good!" he said. It had been all she could do to stay on her feet, but now that she knew what to expect she was ready for him.

She realized, however, that they looked a lot like other couples. And the others were being eliminated like crazy. She knew if Lorenzo saw her as a failure, he would dump her in a minute and then how could she learn more about Alan Trimball?

As a judge headed their way, looking ready to tap Lorenzo on the shoulder and eliminate them, she remembered Michael Jackson's popular moonwalk. Was that from this period? Was it earlier? Maybe later? She had no idea.

As the judge approached, she began moonwalking away from Lorenzo, then toward him. Lorenzo looked surprised, then spun to her side and moonwalked with her. "Where did you learn this crazy step?" he asked.

"Oh...it just came to me, I guess," she said with a smile.

The judge's eyebrows rose in surprise, then he smiled, nodded, and continued on his way eliminating other couples.

They did more side-by-side steps that she remembered seeing in the *Saturday Night* movie that she knew looked good. Lorenzo was especially impressed with the way she looked when she put one arm straight up as she gyrated. He was both surprised and pleased by her dancing, and she guessed the film either hadn't made it to "this" place, or was coming in a later year.

Eventually, few couples remained. Lorenzo was looking desperate.

"Can you go between my legs?" he asked as she danced near.

"Can I what?"

A nearby couple was tapped on the shoulder and eliminated. "Let's go for it!" Lorenzo said, and suddenly grabbed her by the waist, lifted her high over his head, and then in a smooth, steady motion, widened his legs and began to lower her toward the floor.

"Ohmigod," she thought as the music thumped and the strobe lights made it all the more surreal.

All she could think of was to not hit the floor as he swung her down so that her legs went between his. Her butt skidded fast along the slick dance floor, the sateen helping her slide. When she realized her face was headed straight toward his crotch, she dropped her back and head. Lorenzo's hands let go of her waist and gripped her wrists as she zipped through his legs and kept going until her arms were outstretched.

He was bent over nearly double and pulled her back through his legs and then up to a standing position. She scarcely knew what had happened, but she was on her feet, unharmed. The audience roared their approval and applauded.

Good, she thought. Maybe it was time to end this.

But he had a different idea as he spun her again. This time, as she stumbled back toward him, he lowered his body like a football player making a tackle so that her stomach hit him in the shoulder. He hooked an arm around her waist and stood, causing her body to rest on his shoulder like a teeter totter—head and arms on one side, legs on the other.

She lifted her head and legs as he began to spin round and round. The crowd was now clapping and whistling.

She guessed Lorenzo was so energized by that, he suddenly let go of her waist and she rolled off his shoulder, onto the floor. She was face up and just about to turn over to get away from this maniac when he swooped down and he took hold of one ankle and one wrist and started spinning her around and around.

As he spun faster and faster, looking like a deranged whirling dervish, centrifugal force lofted her into the air. A high, fearful wail came from her lips, but no one could hear it because the crowd was roaring its pleasure, cheering and stomping its feet. She feared going into orbit, and knew she was going to throw up if he spun her around one moment longer.

Mercifully, before that happened, Lorenzo became so dizzy he crashed, dropping Angie and causing her to skitter across the dance floor, spinning like a top the whole time, until she smacked into tables and chairs edging the dance floor.

Paavo reached her side. "Wow, Angie! You're a really good dancer!"

Paavo helped Angie limp to his red VW bug, while Lorenzo went off with his First Place ribbon to enjoy the accolades of a number of women. Angie got into the car, but in a flash, she cried out, pushed against the door he was about to close, and jumped out. She stood on the sidewalk, petrified, and pointed toward the car's interior.

Nervously, he peeked inside.

Hanging from the rearview mirror was a little cloth doll. It seemed to be wearing a short skirt and high white boots. It had brown hair...and a knife sticking out of its neck.

Angie sat in Paavo's living room with a blanket around

her shoulders. She began shaking after seeing the hanging doll and hadn't been able to stop.

He was also scared, and it took a long time before he got up nerve to take the doll off the mirror and throw it in the gutter. He tried to act brave, but she saw him quivering.

"It's just some kid playing a prank, that's all," Paavo said after a while. "I'm sure it's nothing to worry about."

"You wouldn't sound half so cavalier if it was you! That doll was me! It was a message! And not a critique of my disco moves. We're getting close to something, and someone knows it!"

"You can't be sure. For one thing, the doll was in my car and looked like several girls I've dated. It was probably one of them putting it in there as a warning to another. Maybe one of them thought you were my latest squeeze."

"Latest *squeeze?*"

"You know how these women are. You, yourself, didn't look all that pleased to hear about me and Nona and we've never even dated." At her murderous glance, he added, "Not yet, anyway."

She turned her head, her eyes shut. She didn't want to think about this faux Paavo. She knew Paavo better than any other person in the world. He had never let anyone else get close to him. He did when he was a boy—he was close to Aulis Kokkonen, his guardian, who raised him after his mother abandoned him and his older sister. But as he grew older, and especially after his sister died, he became ever more guarded until Angie entered his life. Only with her did he learn to let himself be anything other than The Great Stoneface that she first met. With her, he learned to love, to laugh, and to let someone see that he could feel and enjoy and hurt.

Angie loved her taciturn cop, and missed him. This

philandering Romeo was nothing like him. She truly was with a stranger.

"You could stay here tonight, Angie," Paavo said. "No sense you going back to Connie's place. Why disturb her? You're safe here. I'll take care of you. You can even sleep in my bed."

"And you?" she asked.

He smirked. "I'll join you if you'd like."

Angie shook her head. "That won't be necessary." She sat dejected a long moment, then asked for the umpteenth time, "Do you still have no sense that you know me, Paavo?"

"By now, I've been around you so much that I want to say that I do, but being honest, I'd have to say no." He tilted his head and studied her, and slowly his cocky brashness seemed to lift and he spoke honestly. "You wouldn't be an easy person to forget. If we had ever met, I would definitely remember you. That's why I don't understand why no one is looking for you already. They should be. You're...you're a beautiful, smart, interesting woman. A little flaky, I'll admit, but you have a good heart. And you're nice, which is a bit of a shock after Nona. I was starting to think all beautiful women were like her."

"I appreciate the words of flattery, although I still wish you remembered me."

"I'm sorry, Angie."

"So am I. But I would like to stay here," she admitted. "I'm not comfortable around the new Connie."

"New?"

"Forget it. I'm going to bed. Alone. Good-night."

She didn't tell Paavo, but since Plan A had so dismally failed, it was time for Plan B.

Chapter 17

WHILE PAAVO SLEPT the next morning, Angie wrote him a note telling where she was going and why, and asked him to give the information to Connie as well. She then left Paavo's house and took a cab to Nona's apartment. There she packed a bag and picked up Nona's car.

She knew that Connie had to go along with her bosses, and they were fixated on Nona as the most likely killer. Angie disagreed. Something told her that the answer to all this was at the Individual System for Meaning Institute in Mendocino. Nona had been there, Starr was planning to go, and Alan Trimball was fixated on it.

Since no one else would do it, Angie decided it was up to her to learn why.

At 2 p.m., she arrived at the ISMI complex, which sat on the cliffs overlooking the Pacific just outside the small town of Mendocino. The entrance looked like a Japanese garden with high walls and a wooden gate. A new session would begin at 4 p.m. that afternoon. Angie managed to get into it using one of Nona's credit card numbers.

She felt uneasy as she entered, but was welcomed by the perkiest woman she had ever met. Sally had curly hair worn in a Farrah Fawcett cut, a bright lime-colored suit with a short straight mini-skirt and ankle-strap yellow pumps with high heels. Angie was expecting someone who looked like an aging hippie, or possibly one of those bizarre Hari Krishna people, not this activities director type.

She led Angie to the *dojo*, and laughed about *dojo* being the term for a karate studio. That didn't bode well, Angie thought.

Her eight fellow inmates, aka the other students, were standing around drinking coffee and looking extremely nervous, except for a chubby young man with acne and frizzy hair who seemed more interested in the doughnuts than anything else.

"We're all here now," perky Sally said. "Enjoy your coffee and doughnuts because you won't be seeing anything like them for the next three days. You're going to cleanse your body as well as your mind and spirit."

She then gave them keys to their dormitory rooms and sent them off to change their clothes. All came out wearing black pajama-like outfits with wide cotton trousers and bulky hip-length kimono tops that crossed in front and were held together by a sash. On their feet, they wore straw zoris.

The coffee and doughnuts were gone, replaced by nothing. Chubby looked ready to cry.

Instead of perky Sally, a woman of indeterminate age met them. She looked emaciated, wore no make-up, and her skin was badly dried and lined from the sun. Her similarly brittle and lifeless brown hair was parted in the middle and fell in bushy disarray past her shoulders. Her outfit, a sleeveless jumpsuit in a natural linen color, revealed darkly tanned arms without an ounce of fat that looked more like twisted cords of hemp than flesh.

She announced that she was to be known as Seven. Those in the class were forbidden to use their own names. Each was given a two-digit number. Angie found herself named Thirty-five. How boring was that? Chubby ended up Eighty-eight, which to Angie were nice round numbers— much like he was.

Seven brought them to a tatami-floor room where they sat on pillows and listened as one lecturer after the other told them all that was wrong with the world, mankind, and themselves. They spent the next three hours with no bathroom or cigarette breaks, then had a dinner of miso, brown rice, and boiled broccoli, all unflavored or "natural" as the group leader told them. Angie found it basically inedible except for the miso. She spooned some of the soup onto her rice to give it a little flavor.

Suddenly, Seven yelled at her for defiling the rice. Everyone looked shocked. The leader went on and on about how stupid and ignorant Angie was about food, how she shouldn't do such a thing, that she was a vile, awful person, until Angie couldn't take it anymore and told Seven she was being ridiculous.

"You see?" the leader turned to the open-mouthed group. "Number Thirty-five cannot handle the slightest criticism because she has rage against the world and she strikes back. That is the problem with the world today. Innate rage lashes out inappropriately. You are all watching in surprise. When you face anger, hate, irritation or any other negative emotion, you must simply laugh and clap your hands. Let's all try it now."

The group forced themselves to laugh and clap along with Seven. "You, too, Thirty-five."

The leader was a complete looney tunes, Angie thought, but she went along with the foul-tempered pillar of self-righteousness.

"Doesn't everyone feel better?" the leader asked.

"If she's not going to eat that," Eighty-eight pointed at Angie's rice, "can I?"

"No, because you're already too fat," the leader snapped.

At that point, everyone else laughed and clapped.

Eighty-eight lowered his chin to his chest and chased the last couple grains of rice around his plate until he caught and ate them.

Angie didn't know how much more of this she could take.

The second day started out somewhat better than the first in that they were given an egg with their hot rice and tea. One problem, however. The egg was raw. The way to eat it was to mix it with the hot rice and let it cook that way, and this time, it was permissible to pour some of the hot tea onto the egg-rice mixture. Angie would have rather put the egg into the tea kettle to soft boil it, but she knew that would be frowned on. At least the food was edible.

After breakfast, the group walked around the grounds. It was an incredibly lovely two-mile walk. The Mendocino Coast was one of the most beautiful, pristine areas in the entire world, Angie thought, as she and the others viewed the ocean from the cliff tops near the institute. The land dropped sharply into the water and large boulders dotted the shore, jutting high into the sky. When an incoming tide hit those boulders, the spray would shoot into the air. The white spray against the blue sky was gorgeous to behold.

"This is where you will learn to clear your mind of the

world," Seven announced. "To toss it all away. Look at the beauty around you. When you cleanse your mind of all you have learned, you will discover that what you thought was truth is all a lie. There is no truth. Forget the world, its riches and rituals. Even"—she scoffed—"Christmas."

Everyone laughed and clapped.

"Tomorrow, the last day of our class, is the day the unenlightened call Christmas Eve. Some people asked why we have a class that day, when it means you must travel on Christmas Day to your homes. Simple! It's to help you realize that Christmas is a day like any other, and there's no reason to think otherwise.

"When we go out into the world," she continued, "we will praise only nature and ourselves. We worship ourselves, the trees and the rocks. Together, we are nothing, and nothing is the one. That is the individual system of meaning, and we shall teach you to accomplish it!"

Angie shuddered at those words. All in all, she'd rather be with her family and friends celebrating Christmas than here worshipping herself or a rock! She wondered if this was how Pet Rocks started.

The group soon went inside. The morning lecture was about parents, and why everyone in the room was filled with anger. It was all their parents' fault. Parents raised children all wrong. The people of ISMI knew the right way to parent. In fact, they said, they knew the right way to do everything.

Later that morning, Eighty-eight bore the brunt of an attack by Seven about being fat. His parents made him so neurotic he wanted to eat, but he alone shoveled too much food into his mouth. Several others in the class were similarly afflicted. Eighty-eight attempted to stand up for himself, talking about his low metabolism and such. That only sent the class into gales of laughter and clapping.

Angie knew she was supposed to laugh and clap, but she found it difficult. She was appalled that so many people paid no attention to Eighty-eight's feelings.

Soon, Eighty-eight broke down in tears and bolted from the room.

That afternoon, it was Forty-two's turn to be skewered by Seven. Angie had to admit that she wasn't very sympathetic since Forty-two had laughed the loudest at Eighty-eight's misery.

Forty-two was in love with her boss who not only was married, but also was a cad and slept with any woman who gave him the slightest encouragement. The leader screamed at her that for being stupid, that she didn't deserve to be loved, and that the air she breathed was a waste of good oxygen. By the time Seven finished, the woman was a curled up, sniveling mass of angst and misery.

Angie wondered if Seven had ever been in love, or knew what it felt like to be loved.

She saw that Eighty-eight was back in the room and gleefully laughed and applauded at each outrage and each retort Forty-two made to defend herself. Something about this, Angie thought, was really sick—a course in sadism as enlightenment.

She didn't know how sick until later that day when she became the one under attack. By then, she had caught on to the tactic, as she was sure everyone had. The leader wore down the participant's defenses, while the unnatural reaction of the crowd—the clapping and laughing—made the whole thing surreal.

"You are sitting there quietly, Thirty-five," the leader

said.

"Yes. I'm watching," Angie stated.

"You think you're above this, don't you? Why did you come here if you're too good to be a part of it?"

"I'm not too good. I'm just curious."

Seven's thin, dry face contorted with disgust. "You look very stupid sitting and saying nothing. You don't like the way this session is going, do you?"

"I didn't say that."

"Perhaps you should be leading it. You think you know everything already, don't you?"

"One thing I do know," Angie said calmly, "is that you're no better than Eighty-eight or Forty-two or me."

"And how do you speak with such authority?" Seven asked with a sneer.

"Because I know ISMI will never amount to anything. Years from now, no one will have heard of it."

The leader faced the other students. "She is stupid as well as arrogant."

The class laughed and clapped.

Angie didn't let any of this bother her. "I see how fake everything here is."

Seven grew angry. "You are nothing! You know nothing!"

"Don't I? Eighty-eight is just a shill, isn't he?" Angie said. "Your job was too easy with him. You said a few words and he went into a rage and then cried and ran off—all the things you've told people to expect at ISMI sessions. I'll bet he comes to each of these sessions, and his payment is probably all the doughnuts he wants. In each session you'll find people who are thinking, 'well, at least I'm not Eighty-eight.' This whole thing is a scam to make money!"

Seven pursed her lips. "I feel sorry for you, Thirty-five.

We are here to help people. We might have been able to help you, except that you're afraid to listen to us. What are you afraid you might hear? Something about you not being as pretty or as smart or as perfect as you think you are? You're nothing but a cheap little nobody trying to pretend you're someone special. I'll bet your friends laugh at you behind your back—if you have any friends."

"I have friends," Angie said, although she was struck by the realization that she had no real friends in this world.

"Is that so? Then, where are they? You're all alone in the world and you're trying to take it out on ISMI, when all you have to do is accept that you're nothing, and that the whole world is against you. It is against you, isn't it? Isn't it?"

"It's not." Angie said. But the thought of how she found herself here, in this strange time, all alone...

"Nobody cares about you, Thirty-five. Admit it! Nobody cares what you do, what you say, or what you think. They've all abandoned you, haven't they?"

"No!" Her heart beat faster.

"You're lying! You can lie to yourself but not to me. Not to all of us. We can see through you. You're nothing! You do nothing! No one gives a damn what happens to you. If you were to die, no one would miss you, no one would care! Admit it! Admit it, now!"

"Stop it!"

"Face it. You, your life, is meaningless!"

"No, I'm someone in my world."

"This *is* your world!"

"No! Never! All this...it's a dream. A nightmare!"

The class stopped laughing altogether, and Seven looked at her as if she were crazy. "You're delusional."

Angie stood. "You believe that the ego is the most

important part of man, that what 'I' want and how 'I' see the world is all that matters. You say there is no truth, but you're wrong. Truth has nothing to do with you or me. It's part of the world and bigger than any of us or all of us together. When you forget that, you raise Man to the level of God, and that's where you fall apart because, ultimately, man simply isn't good enough. And that's the fallacy behind everything you're doing and saying."

"You know nothing about it!" Seven insisted.

"I know I don't want to watch you tear down others. It's cruel, and doesn't teach anyone a single thing about themselves or how to make their lives better."

With that, Angie walked to the door to leave. The classroom laughed and applauded as if she were a stand-up comedian. She shook her head and didn't even turn around.

Chapter 18

ANGIE WAS USHERED into the office of Hans Olaf Gerling, the founder of ISMI.

He was a surprisingly young man. She expected him to be wizened and German, but he was about 5'8" and surprisingly husky for someone who should be eating the type of food served to his students. His brown hair was quite long and scraggly, and he wore a caftan, jeans, and Birkenstocks without socks.

"You asked to see me, Miss Amalfi?"

"Yes. I wanted to see who I was paying to be insulted. I didn't understand that was the game being played when I came here, Mr. Gerling."

"Please, call me Hans. May I call you Angie?"

"I couldn't care less."

"Very good!" he said with a smile. He looked as if he was about to clap, but changed his mind. "Sit please." He gestured toward soft leather chairs. She sat in one, he sat facing her.

"This is no game," he explained. "It has to do with RAGE—Righteous Anger Generates Equilibrium. People are afraid of their own anger, you see. That's what the problem is. It builds and builds inside us until it actually makes us ill. At ISMI we first bring that anger to the surface, get you to recognize it so that you can release it, and finally, to rise above it and find a state of equilibrium...of balance. We have a wonderful program here, and I think you're exactly the type of person who would benefit very much. You have a lot going for you, Angie. I can see that. In fact, it's almost dinner time. Will you join me?"

"For miso and boiled rice? What goes with it tonight, cabbage?"

He gave her an indulgent smile. "One of the things we do at ISMI is to wear you down physically as well as emotionally. The food you're given is enough to sustain you. There is definite nutritious value in all we serve, but it leaves most Westerners unsatisfied. Your cravings for meat, chocolate, caffeine, and so on, aren't being met. That's another reason why people are so quick to anger. But you're angry enough. You don't need to starve tonight. In fact, if you promise not to tell, there's a very good house of prime rib in town. You can get a baked potato with all the trimmings with it, and they do an excellent crème brûlée for dessert."

She didn't have to think twice. "Mr. Gerling, you've got a date."

After dinner, Hans walked Angie back to her dormitory. They had spent most of their time together with him talking about himself—his philosophy, how he began ISMI, how it had grown and made him a very wealthy man, but (he quickly added) his spiritual growth, not economic, was the real benefit of all he did here—his own spiritual growth as well as that of the students who benefitted from the seminars.

When they neared the rooms, Hans took her hand in both of his. "I must leave you here so no one sees us together. It's bad enough that we have to tear down people's self-esteem; we don't want them to think that the staff plays favorites besides."

"I'm a favorite now?"

He lifted her hand and kissed the back of it, then continued to hold it. "You are charming. Definitely a favorite. But I can also see that you're hiding something. I've never known a person with so much caution. You intrigue me, Angie. There's something that's different about you. Something very knowing. I have no idea what it is. But whatever it is, I do like it. I want you to know that."

He moved a little closer, and she backed away.

"Thank you," she said. "You've made this experience much easier for me. I understand everything a lot more clearly."

"Good."

She pulled her hand free. "Good-bye, Hans."

He grabbed her arm as she tried to turn from him. "I'll see you tomorrow, Angie. After the other students leave, my time will be much freer, as I hope yours will as well."

"Yes," she whispered, not liking how tightly he gripped her. "Of course." With that she jerked her arm free and hurried into the dormitory.

Chapter 19

IT WAS ONLY SIX a.m., but it was the first time Connie was able to reach Angie by phone after a day of being told she "wasn't available."

"Don't do anything that will cause you to stand out from the other students," Connie ordered.

"What do you mean?" Angie asked.

"I'm coming up there with Stan Bonnette—he's been a big part of the research we've been doing. Also, Paavo will join us. He's worried about you. I think he cares about you. A lot. So just sit tight, okay? We'll be there as soon as we can."

"Sure," Angie said. "But can't you tell me what's going on?"

"It's a long story. They're waiting for me to leave. Keep away from Gerling. We've discovered he's really Peter Lemon, another of Starr's students. The name Gerling didn't exist until three years ago when ISMI started. We're on our way, but in the meantime, be careful."

As Angie hung up, she realized Hans Olaf Gerling, aka Peter Lemon, must be the one behind the killings. No one could be that slimy and be innocent. The problem was, she had no idea why he did it. Or, frankly, how.

Thinking of Connie's caution not to draw attention to herself, Angie went back to class. She acted ashamed of her actions the day before, which seemed to please Seven to a disgusting degree. The morning was even more hideous than the day before because most of the students agreed that they were, in fact, nothing. Now, Seven needed to fill them with meaning the ISMI way. What she actually filled them with was the need to sign up for ISMI's "infusion" class, five days, starting the second week of January.

During morning break, Angie was hurrying back to her room to see if she had received any more calls or messages from Connie, when Hans Gerling approached her.

"Mr. Gerling," she said, surprised.

"After last evening, I should think you'd call me Hans." He clasped both her hands and kissed her cheek. "I couldn't wait until this evening to see you again."

"Oh, well..." She looked around. No one was near. "I was going to get a sweater and then go back to class."

He put an arm around her shoulders and turned her away from the dormitory. "Come with me. You'll learn more from me than in today's class. And I've got a nice fire going in my home."

"Your home?"

"Yes. I live on the grounds, you know. But my home is private. No one will bother us there."

Oh, dear!

Hans' home was small but plush. The west side was a wall of windows looking out on the ocean. The north wall was rock-faced and included a large fireplace with built-in bookshelves on each side.

"This is beautiful," Angie said.

They stood at the window admiring the view. "Yes," he said. "I appreciate all I've done for myself every day when I look out and see this."

For a moment, she thought she heard him incorrectly. She realized she hadn't.

"That's the ISMI way, I guess." She smiled.

"Absolutely. Our mantra: *The one who does everything for me, who loves me, and cares for me, ISMI!*" With that, he laughed and put his arms around her, pulling her close. "By the way, I heard someone phoned you yesterday, and again this morning. We don't normally allow our students to be interrupted by the outside world, but when she said she was from the San Francisco Police Department..."

Angie saw the hardness lurking in his eyes even as he smiled down at her. "Oh, that was nothing. She's a friend. I called her when I was upset yesterday and told her I was leaving. She was worried when I didn't make it back to the city last night."

"A friend?" he asked.

"I do have them," she said with a smile, "no matter what Seven thinks."

He laughed and his arms tightened. "We don't like the police getting involved in the good work we do here," he said. "It made me curious about you. I asked around and learned you work at Nona's with some of my friends. And that you ask a lot of questions."

Lorenzo! She thought. Lorenzo was working with Gerling! She pulled free of him and backed away. She smiled as she said, "My questions led me to ISMI—to experience what a fine program this is."

"Is that why you went to talk to Mary Jacobson?" His

face turned fierce.

Maria? Had her own sister told Gerling about her questions? She couldn't speak.

"You wanted to know about Professor Starr," Gerling said. "I think you are arriving at some very erroneous conclusions, Angie."

"Not at all," she cried.

"You're not a good liar."

She swallowed. He was right. "I...I learned Professor Starr would give his classes projects on what outrageous thing people might be not only willing to do, but would pay to do." She decided to take a leap—some of the information she had learned, and others she had extrapolated. "ISMI was developed in one of those classes. It was Alan Trimball's class project. He apparently kept carbon copies of the term paper he submitted to Professor Starr, and Starr may still have the originals."

He laughed. "So that's what this is all about."

"I know your name is Peter Lemon. You were in that class and you heard Alan Trimball's oral presentation of his idea. You knew it could work."

He folded his arms. "This is madness. The idea for ISMI came to me in a dream—a mescaline-induced dream, if you must know. I worked all of it out on my own, with no help. I'm the creator. There's no doubt about it."

"What happened? Was Alan going to sue you? I heard he was planning a lawsuit."

"Sue me? Hah! He would have to get in line. I get threatened with suits all the time."

She backed towards the door. "The police"—she had to divert his attention away from her—"the police think you killed Trimball."

He laughed. "What do they know? I've never killed

anyone!" He remained calm and controlled.

"They also think you killed Professor Starr. Starr knew Trimball was telling the truth. He may have even kept Trimball's class papers to help prove his case."

"What!" He frowned, suddenly perplexed. "Are you saying Starr was murdered?"

His question stunned her. "Of course."

"But the newspapers...they've been quiet about what happened to Starr, saying they were waiting for results from the autopsy. I assumed he had a heart attack or something."

"The police kept the cause of death quiet on purpose," Angie said. "Both men were poisoned with the same food."

He stared at her as if he couldn't believe what he was hearing. "Poisoned...both? So that means whoever did it had to have access to that food, and also be trusted enough by both men." He paled. "Oh, my God! I know who did it!"

If he was lying, Angie thought, he was quite convincing. "Who?" she asked.

"Let me call the guards at the gate. He's coming here! They can't let him in! I—we—could be in danger."

"Who?" Angie insisted as Gerling picked up the phone.

He banged on the hook several times. "It's dead! He may be here already!"

"That's ridiculous," Angie said.

From the door came another voice. "Is it?"

Angie spun around. The first thing she saw was the handgun pointed at her and Gerling. Then she looked up. "You!"

Connie told the guard at the gate that she, Paavo and Stan had a meeting with Gerling. The guard phoned his home office, but received no answer.

"He's probably waiting for us outside," Connie said, and showed her badge. "We want to be let in. Now."

"I'm sorry," the guard said. "Just give me a moment to—"

A shot rang out from Gerling's residence.

The three plus the guard ran toward it.

Connie drew her gun.

All was silent.

She steeled herself as best she could even though the idea of confronting potential killers frightened her so much she could scarcely breathe. But she wore the uniform of a cop. Somehow, she could do it.

The security guard, a fairly old man, said, "I'll make sure the students don't come this way."

Connie nodded, then tiptoed toward the house, her gun aimed and ready to fire.

Chapter 20

"DON'T SHOOT!" ANGIE screamed, looking with horror at Gerling's body lying on the floor, blood flowing fast from a wound to the chest. "You need me to get out of this alive!"

"It's too late!"

"No! I'm sure you can explain everything. You're a smart man, Winslow," Angie said. "I wondered why you were working as a dishwasher even though you went to law school. That's what this is about, isn't it?"

He extended his arm, stretching the gun closer to her. "You know too much!"

"Make me your hostage!" Angie shouted. "If you kill me, what will stop the sheriff and his deputies, or whoever is the law up here, from bursting in with their guns blazing? I know you don't want to die. You did all this to save yourself, didn't you? I think, if you tell your story, people will understand. There be extenuating circumstances. I know you. You aren't a bad person! You might get off with just a little time, and then you can go on with your life."

"It's all gone wrong," he cried, his face reddening with emotion. She didn't know if he was going to burst into tears or shoot her.

"Tell me about it," she said. "Please, Winslow. We've talked at the restaurant. You're no killer. Tell me, are you married? Do you have a family?"

He shook his head. "I'm not. Just my parents and my brother and sister."

"Your parents must be very proud of you, being a lawyer and all."

"They used to be."

"If you get killed, think of them," Angie pleaded. "Today is Christmas Eve. How would they feel if you were killed the day before Christmas?"

A tear began to roll down his cheek.

"Why has all this happened to you, Winslow?" She thought about the fact that he was able to get past security. That meant he had to be known to the guards. That meant...she gasped. "You're Hans Gerling's attorney, aren't you? Or should I say Peter Lemon's?"

Winslow nodded. He relaxed his hand with the gun a bit, but still pointed it at her. "He changed his name to Hans Olaf Gerling when he founded ISMI. He got the idea of coming up with that kind of name after seeing the success Werner Erhart had with EST. People will shell out money to someone with a name like Hans Olaf Gerling a lot faster than someone named Lemon."

"Yes, I think he was right about that," Angie said.

Winslow scowled. "It was the only thing he was right about! The man was a fool! A pothead. I saw how much money Gerling was making, and that he was wasting it on drugs. If it weren't for me, he'd have nothing. I invested it for him, and built this compound into what it is today."

"But now you've shot him…and"—she didn't want to use the word 'murder'—"you've eliminated two others as well. Why, Winslow?"

He began to shake. Angie gasped as the gun wriggled. She hoped it didn't have a hair trigger. "They would have messed things up!" he said on the verge of blubbering. She realized he was talking about Trimball and Starr. "They wanted to take this to court, to make me open my books to the world. No one would understand that I had to borrow some of Gerling's money. I had to! Do you know how expensive it is to get a law degree?"

Winslow stopped a moment to wipe the tears from his eyes. "I had bills while Gerling had all *this*…thanks to me! I learned Trimball would not only file a lawsuit, but his professor would back him up! Professor Starr apparently gave Alan guidance as he developed his project, and now believed he deserved partial ownership of it! Alan agreed with him. Between the two of them, they would have bled Gerling dry. And me."

"That's why you took the dishwasher job?" Angie asked, trying to put the pieces together.

"I hoped to learn Alan was just boasting, and didn't really mean what he was saying. I wasn't anywhere near that stupid sociology class, I was over in the law school taking real classes! But I soon saw that Alan was serious, and he seemed to have all the proof he needed."

"So how did Nona Farraday get involved in all this?"

Winslow shrugged. "It just happened. At one point, before I knew Starr was involved, I tried to simply steal his school papers, but he must have put them in a safe deposit box or hid them some place. When I couldn't find them, I knew Alan would realize his apartment had been broken into, so I stole his recipe collection to give him something to focus on that had nothing to do with ISMI."

Angie nodded. "So that's why, when you decided to kill him and Starr, you went with one of the recipes from the restaurant and added arsenic to it. But how did you get them to eat it?"

"That was easy. I heated up a bowl of poisoned food and told Alan that I saw Nona cooking it. I thought it was really delicious, and if she kept cooking so well, she might not need him much longer. Then I said she must have used some odd spice because I couldn't tell what it was, but it made the food really tasty. That was enough to pique the interest of a chef. He took the bowl from me and put a spoonful in his mouth. He said it did have something odd in it, but he couldn't tell what it was. By the third mouthful, he was feeling ill. I encouraged him to take another couple of bites and then got him out to my car before he passed out. I rolled him into an alley near Nona's apartment."

"Clever," Angie said, well understanding both the jealousy and curiosity chefs have about each other's recipes.

She noticed that the doorknob on the office door appeared to be slowly turning. She raised her voice—"But what about Starr? How did it work for Starr?"—just as someone pushed the door open a sliver of an inch.

"Starr took even more cleverness on my part, if I do say so. I delivered a 'home-cooked meal' to him, saying it was from Alan. Fortunately, he ate it. I suspected he would—a single man, retired. I suspected if he could avoid having to cook for himself one night, he would do so."

"You're definitely clever, Winslow," Angie said.

"But not clever enough to keep out of trouble!" he cried. "Let's go. It's still quiet here. I thought that gunshot might draw the security guard, but obviously, he's paying no attention. We're going to go for a ride. Don't make a fuss, and I'll let you go as soon as I get across the Canadian border."

As he walked toward her, she sidled along the wall of the office, inching nearer the door.

"Don't do that, Angie!" he said as he stepped closer to the door, facing her and blocking the exit. "You've cooperated so far, and it was your idea to use you as a hostage, so don't make me hurt you now."

"I really don't feel like going to Canada," she said. "Let's talk about this some more."

"We're done talking," he said. "Now, move it!" He reached for her arm. Angie dropped to the floor and dived behind the sofa just as the door behind him burst open. Paavo barreled into him, knocking him half-way across the room, and sending the gun flying.

Angie didn't come out until she heard Connie make the arrest.

Paavo rushed Angie to the dormitory for her few belongings and then to Nona's car. He took the car keys from her—she was in no shape to drive—and immediately headed back to San Francisco.

He and Connie had discussed this on the way up. If everything went according to plan, Connie didn't want Angie to make any statements to the Mendocino police. Statements from a crazy woman could cause more problems to the case than they would solve at this moment. Later, they could decide what to do about her.

Stan was willing to go along if they would convince Angie to give him an exclusive interview of all she saw and did while at ISMI. They agreed to try.

Connie needed to stay in Mendocino for a while to work out jurisdictional issues. Hans Gerling would survive, the gunshot wasn't fatal, but Winslow would have a number of charges in Mendocino for attempted murder as well as embezzlement. Those paled compared to the two murder charges he would face in San Francisco.

Connie's mentor, Inspector Bruce Whalen, was driving up to Mendocino help her deal with both charges and jurisdiction. He also told her he didn't think it was right that she would have to spend Christmas alone.

oOo

Angie leaned back against the car seat and shut her eyes. She was glad Connie wouldn't be alone, and judging from the happy, rosy-cheeked way Connie talked about her mentor, something else might be at work there, even if Connie didn't know it yet.

But Angie had no idea what her own future held. She felt great relief that the murders were solved, and that she hadn't been killed in the process. If she thought proving Nona innocent would help her find her way back to her own reality, however, looking at 'Polyester Paavo' singing "Groovin' on a Sunday Afternoon" along with the radio, that wasn't happening.

Chapter 21

BACK IN HIS apartment, Paavo poured them each a glass of Chablis, and then put a record on the turntable. Soon, Nat King Cole was singing about chestnuts roasting on an open fire.

Paavo took Angie's hand and led her to the couch where he kissed her. She melted into his kiss for a moment, then pushed back. Gently, she rested her hand against the side of his face. "You're a good man, Paavo Smith, but I don't belong here."

"You don't have to go anywhere. Stay with me, Angie." He took her in his arms again. "I think you're crazier than a bed bug, but it doesn't matter. Nothing matters as long as we're together. I don't care if you say you're from the future, or another planet, or even if in a former life you were Cleopatra. I'm falling in love with you."

"I'm so sorry, Paavo. I don't know what to do, but I can't make a life here."

"If you leave, I'll have no one."

"You've got Nona," Angie said.

He shook his head. "I like her, but it's not love. I know Nona doesn't love me. It sounds harsh, but I think she's too much in love with herself to see anything love-worthy in another person. Does that make sense to you, Angie?"

His phone began to ring.

"It does. If she's missing out on a good man like you because of being self-centered, I'm very sorry for her." The ringing continued. "Are you going to answer?"

"I don't care who it is. No one is as important to me as being here with you. It's as if I lived in shadow, and now there's sunshine. To me, you've made all the difference."

The answering machine clicked on.

—*Paavo, it's Nona. I'm being freed! The police found the real killer. They're letting me go. I'm taking a taxi home. Come and see me, darling. I've missed you. I've missed you very*—

At that, the tape ran out.

Paavo caught Angie's eyes, then he dropped his gaze.

Angie took his hand. "You should go see her."

"Is it fair to her, when you're the one I want to be with?" he asked. "Although why that is when I hardly know you, I have no idea."

"I'm sorry, Paavo," she said.

"I see how you look at me, Angie. You can't look at someone like that and then deny that they're special to you. I don't know what any of this means, or where it'll lead, or even why it's happening. I only know I want you to be a part of my life."

His words cut through her. There was much to this man that was lovable, but he wasn't her Paavo. He had potential, but he wasn't the full measure of the man. She looked away.

"We'll work it out, Angie," he said. "We'll see some doctors, find out what's wrong. In time, I'm sure you'll get over this idea of being from the future. You're the sanest person I know, so I can't explain what's happened to you, but whatever it is, it doesn't matter. I don't want to lose you!"

"Don't, Paavo. Please. This is wrong."

"No! It's the most right thing I've ever done or felt."

Her heart was breaking as she stood up and put on her coat. "Go to Nona. She cares about you, she really does. She tries to bully her way through life, always the tough person who pretends she isn't bleeding on the inside, but she often is. That's why it's necessary to let her know she's loved and appreciated. Sometimes people pretend that they're strong because they're afraid to show how vulnerable they are. I've always believed that explained Nona. She can be a bitch, but there's a soft side too. I guess that's why, despite the fact that I'm usually fighting with her, deep, deep down, I actually...kinda sorta...do like her."

He grimaced. "That isn't much of an endorsement."

"Maybe not, but it's the best I can do. Oh, and suggest she make Greg Reed her next chef. He's really quite talented."

Paavo nodded, even as his gaze turned sad. "Where will you go, Angie?"

"I don't know. But I've got to try to find my way back."

"How are you going to do it?"

"I don't know that either. But I have no choice."

She turned toward the door and opened it.

"Tomorrow's Christmas," he said. "Surely you don't want to be alone on Christmas. You should stay here. Wait until the new year."

She shook her head. "I'm afraid if I stay too long, I may never be able to go back. And I do want to be home for Christmas."

"In case you can't get there," he said. "I'll be here

waiting for you, here and now."

"Good-bye, Paavo." She put the extra set of Nona's keys on the small table by the door. "Give Nona my best."

With that, she turned and walked out of the house.

She stood on the bluff at Land's End looking out at the Pacific, at the beauty and vastness and endlessness of it. She had no idea what to do. She ached to go back home, but couldn't. To think otherwise was to cause herself endless sorrow.

The sound of a saxophone again drifted her way. Her strange friend. She walked deeper into the park.

Tim Burrows sat on the ground between the pathway and the cliff's edge playing *Morning has Broken*. For a reason she couldn't name, it seemed an odd choice, and put her nerves on edge. But then, everything seemed to these days.

She walked over to him and sat. When the song ended, he turned to her.

"You look unhappy," he said, leaning closer.

"Yes. I don't know how I'll ever get back to my family and friends. I can't bear it any longer."

"Maybe I can help you."

"I don't think so."

He rested the saxophone on the ground. "Yes, beautiful lady, I can."

His words...beautiful lady...where had she...?

Oh, God!

He took a switchblade from his pocket, and pressed a button. A long blade sprang forward.

"What's that?" Angie said, scrambling to her feet. "What are you doing with it?"

He jumped up, standing between her and the path. "This is the way I can help." His voice was soft, almost soothing. "I've helped many others, you know. Men as well as women. Some in lover's lanes. Some alone."

Men. Women. Lover's lanes...

"I...I don't..." Angie couldn't think, but just babbled. This couldn't be how it would end. Here, alone, away from everyone she held dear. She stepped backwards, towards the cliff's rim, wondering if there was a way she could climb down it.

He picked up the sax and slowly, steadily walked towards her. She ran to the edge, but it was a sheer drop. She froze, unable to take another step without falling. He dropped the sax as he lunged at her, grabbing her arms, his fingers like steel. She fought, pushing against him, praying they didn't both plunge to the rocks far below.

At that moment the earth gave a violent, side-to-side jolt that knocked Tim and Angie to the ground. He let her go as he fell. As she scrambled to crawl away from him her foot accidentally kicked the sax, sending it spinning towards the cliff's edge.

Tim got up and ran to his horn, grabbing it just before it went over, but the quake knocked him down again, this time even closer to the brink. He tried to find a foothold, but the soft, loose rock crumbled beneath him, causing his legs to slip over the lip of the cliff.

Tim held the neck of the horn with one hand, and the other clutched a handful of scrub brush. He stretched the sax towards her.

"Pull me up!" he ordered. His eyes, his demeanor were no longer the harmless, rather slow man he pretended to be.

Angie lay flat on her stomach, the ground solid

beneath her and no longer shaking. One hand held a shrub and with the other she reached out and took hold of the bell of the saxophone. But then she stopped.

He was the Zodiac. And he wanted to kill her. The police were wrong about his description, about the type of man he was. No wonder they could never find him! If she helped him, how many more innocent people would he go on to kill?

"Pull, I said!"

"You like killing people," she cried. "How does it feel to be close to death?"

"Damn you! Help me!"

His weight slowly caused the clump of scrub he held to lift up from the ground.

Still, she did nothing. Her heart pounded harder. *Let go of the saxophone!* her mind cried, but she couldn't do it. Instead, she remained still, holding the bell so tightly her fingers began to ache.

The tuft of scrub ripped free of the earth. With that, he finally let go of the horn and flailed for something to hold, a shrub, rock, anything. His body seemed to hover a moment, and then disappeared.

There was a single splash in the water, and then nothing.

Angie inched her way to the edge of the cliff.

The water swept him far from the rocky shore. When she saw him reappear, he was face down, lifelessly bobbing, until the waves pulled him under once more. She watched and watched for what seemed like an eternity, but he was gone.

The ground began to shake again.

"No!" she cried, clutching the saxophone tight against her chest.

Then all turned quiet for just a moment until...

She heard chimes playing Lohengrin's Wedding March.

She screamed.

Chapter 22

A NGIE! IT'S ALL right! Angie!"
She opened her eyes to hear her cell phone
ringing. She had made "The Wedding March" her latest
ringtone. Paavo was standing over her. And, thanks be to
God, his bushy hair and mutton-chop sideburns were gone.

She saw her mother and father, her sisters Bianca,
Caterina, and Maria, her neighbor, Stan Bonnette, and her
dear friend Connie—again with short, fluffy blond hair and
wearing cream colored slacks and a yellow jacket instead of
a policeman's uniform—all standing around the bed she
was in, looking drawn and worried.

Her fourth sister, Frannie, had answered Angie's cell
phone and was now talking quietly.

She was in a room filled with equipment.

"Angelina?" her mother said. "Can you hear us?"

She reached up and felt strange things stuck to her
forehead, saw tubes and needles jabbed under the skin of
her hand. "What's all this?"

"We had an earthquake," Paavo said, taking her hand
in his as he sat at her side. "We think a branch from a tree
in Washington Square hit you on the head and gave you a

concussion. You were out cold for hours."

Her hands immediately went to her hair as thoughts of her head being shaved struck. Thank heavens, it was all there.

"She'll be okay," her sister Frannie said, "since she cares more about damage to her hair than to her brains. That was Nona, by the way. She was wondering how you're doing."

"Nona? Is she all right?" Angie asked.

"Yeah. She's the one who saw what happened to you. She was late for the hairdresser's and was running through the park when the earthquake hit. She noticed that you didn't get up when everyone else did, and called nine-one-one, then Paavo. He let the rest of us know."

"Nona did that for me?" Angie murmured. "Who would have thought it?"

"She's not that bad," Paavo said. "Anyway, the doctors told us your vitals are fine and there was no significant internal swelling, although you've got quite a goose egg on your head. For some reason, though, you simply would not wake up."

"I think it was a trauma-induced coma," Caterina said knowingly. She always had an answer.

"There's no such thing," Bianca, the most practical sister, exclaimed.

The most mysterious—some would say spooky—sister, Maria, added, "I felt that you were somewhere else, and it took a while for you to come back to us."

Her mother brushed Angie's hair off her forehead and looked at her lovingly. "I told them you decided it was a way to take a rest after all the running around you've been doing. I wasn't worried at all!"

"Not much!" Sal's voice was gruff with emotion, his

eyes teary, as he looked at the baby of the family in a hospital bed.

"What about the earthquake?" Angie asked. "Did it do much damage."

"My shop's a mess," Connie said. "But it's insured. Maybe with the insurance money, I'll be able to get a second chance at making a go of it."

"Lots of minor damage," Paavo said. "No loss of life, but lots of people hurt...like you."

"Well, aside from a horrible headache," Angie said. "I should go home and let someone who needs it have this bed."

"They would like you to stay here overnight for observation," Paavo said. "I'll stay with you, then I'll take you home."

"And the rest of us will leave you two alone so Angie can get her strength back," Serefina added. "You gave us a good scare, Angelina. Don't you dare do it again!"

After kisses and hugs, everyone left.

"How do you really feel?" Paavo asked.

"Fine, honestly. But I need to know one thing—did the police ever find out who the Zodiac killer was or what happened to him?"

"The Zodiac?" Paavo looked at her strangely. "No one knows. Sometime in the mid-seventies or so he suddenly stopped taunting the police and newsmen, and as far as we know, killed no one else. No one ever knew why."

"That's what I thought," Angie said, sitting up. "Did anyone ever suspect a man named Tim Burrows?"

"Not that I remember," Paavo said. "But I haven't read up on the case for years. I'll look into it for you, if you'd like."

"Yes, please!" she spoke quickly. "Could you do it now?

Burrows was a vet, Air Force, and his mother lived in Santa Rosa—if he really existed, that is."

"Angie, calm yourself. What is this about?"

"Uh...nothing. Just curious." She smiled.

Paavo gave her a worried glance, but went ahead and called his partner. Yosh was still at work. After a while, Paavo hung up. "Well, Burrows did exist. The police never suspected him of being the Zodiac, but one reporter did give them his name saying someone suggested he might be the killer. In any case, his mother claimed he disappeared some time in 1975. No one ever knew what happened to him. Now tell me, why are you suddenly asking about all this?"

She debated a moment about how much to tell him. Then decided...not much. "I had the strangest dream. I must have read something about the Zodiac years ago and it came back to me while I was out of it."

It had to have been a dream, she thought. Just a strange dream. She wondered why she had dreamed it.

"Are you sure you're all right?" he asked.

"Yes, now that you're here."

He bent over and lightly kissed her.

She put her arms around him. It felt good to hold him. She hadn't really gone back to the 1970s, of course, although she had to admit that the thought of going back in time, or to a parallel universe, or wherever in the world (or out of it) she was, and helping her friends was pretty satisfying. After all, if she hadn't gone back and didn't press to save Nona, would Nona have been falsely charged with murder? Would Connie have joined the People's Temple? Would Stan have been in the mayor's office on that fateful day? And, perhaps most of all, would the Zodiac have killed a lot more people until someone finally put together who he was and stopped him?

Of course, none of it had actually happened. It was all a dream, a crazy dream.

It truly was more than her poor brain could handle.

What she could handle was being home again. Why had she ever thought Christmas was a bother? She realized its true importance—that through it, she could remember that nothing was more important than the people she loved, whether she was with them or not.

She let go of Paavo and lay back down. "Merry Christmas, Paavo," she whispered, holding his hand.

"Merry Christmas, Angie."

Just then, a nurse came in wheeling a cart.

"Sorry to interrupt," she said to Angie. "I thought you'd want these." From the cart, she pulled the shopping bag filled with Christmas presents ready for the post office and placed it on the counter by the window, and then she took out an old, somewhat dented saxophone, and put it on top of the bag. "I've never seen anything like it," the nurse said, her hand lingering a moment on the sax. "Even though you were unconscious when you were wheeled into Emergency, you were hugging this horn for dear life. I guess it's important to you."

Then she smiled at Angie, and walked out of the room.

Angie stared at the sax a long moment before she murmured, "Oh. My. God."

The
Thirteenth
Santa

IT WAS CHRISTMAS EVE and Homicide Inspector Rebecca Mayfield was on a case.

Garlands of silver tinsel and strings of cheery lights decorated the open parking lot of San Francisco's largest mall. In the center of it, while curious shoppers gawked and impatient drivers raged over the loss of parking spaces, yellow crime scene tape surrounded a black body bag. Homicide detectives were put in charge when a suspicious death occurred, and as soon as Rebecca arrived the concerned merchants of Stonestown descended on her, screaming their outrage over the distasteful police presence. A corpse could dampen tidings of good cheer under the best of circumstances, they protested, but to see one at high noon on the day before Christmas would cause shoppers to flee to the competition.

Frankly, surveying the crowd, it didn't appear as if anyone much cared.

Earlier, as she drove to the mall in answer to the SFPD dispatcher's call, she'd worried about the crime scene because of both the day and the location. She hoped the death would have a simple and obvious explanation—bad health, for example. Joggers, in particular, were big on dropping like flies in the damnedest locations.

Given the strange smirks on the faces of the patrol cops who guarded the body, though, she had the badfeeling that there'd be nothing at all normal about this case.

Officer Mike Hennings was a friend from the Taraval Station. Like her, he was single and therefore a prime candidate for holiday duty. They'd dated a couple of times until both realized it wasn't going to work. Maybe it was because as a homicide inspector, she was superior to him. Or maybe something else. She didn't know, and preferred not to analyze it.

"What's so funny, Mike?" She pushed back the sides of her black wool blazer, her hands on the hips of her black slacks as she surveyed the area. The air was crisp, the sky pale blue. Gulls swarmed overhead awaiting discarded food from overfed, harried shoppers. "You guys look ready to split your guts about something."

Officer Hennings' eyes darted toward his partner. His mustache twitched in his effort to keep a straight face. "There's nothing funny, Rebecca. A man's death is never amusing."

His partner sputtered and clamped a hand over his mouth. Rebecca glared. The more he tried not to laugh, the more his shoulders shook.

"You're right, Mike." Rebecca flipped open her pocket notebook. "A man's death is a grave matter."

Hennings' partner stomped his foot, and doubled over from his struggles.

"Remove the sheet, please," she ordered.

Hennings carefully lifted it away, reversing the direction he'd placed it over the body to cause minimal disruption to any evidence.

Even being a cop, the sight jarred her at first, then calmly, she studied the victim. He lay next to a dumpster like a bloodied, broken rag doll. Apparently, he'd only been discovered because the scavenger company had come by to remove the overflowing trash bin.

His bones were twisted at unnatural angles and his body seemed oddly squished, as if he'd fallen from a great height. She looked up and then all around. They were in an open parking lot. No buildings were near. There was nothing for him to have fallen *from*.

That was when she realized what had amused the cops. Even before Hennings spoke the words, she could predict what he was going to say. "It looks like"—he began before, like his partner, he sputtered and chuckled—"it looks like he fell off his sleigh."

"He hit the eject button by mistake," his partner blurted.

"Santa the sky-diver." Hennings howled.

As the two rolled around with laughter, Rebecca made no reply. It was Christmas Eve, and Santa Claus—red suit, tasseled hat, black boots and all—lay at her feet, dead.

"What the hell! Damnation!" Richie Amalfi stomped back and forth over an empty parking space, gesturing wildly. A short while ago the space was filled by a monstrous white Ford Econoline passenger van. And the van was filled with twelve Very Important People. But now, it—and its passengers—were gone. "I don't believe it!" he bellowed with rage.

Wasn't it bad enough that he, a man who usually saw the light of dawn as he was going to bed, had to face it this morning when he got up? Now, the whole reason he had roused himself at an ungodly hour had blown up. He should have stayed home. Bed, booze and broads—they were what made life worth living. And his life wasn't going to be worth squat if he didn't solve this present problem.

He ran both hands through his black hair. His eyeballs bulged; his scalp felt like it was being squeezed.

It was nearly Christmas. Filled with good cheer, he had agreed to handle this little task. Now, his Christmas spirit was going to get him a .45 through the brain.

That morning at the San Francisco airport he'd picked up his charges one-by-one as they arrived from different parts of the country. The first was there at seven, the last at ten. The four who'd come in from the east coast had arrived the night before and stayed at an airport hotel.

Like some little Mary Sunshine googly-eyed social director he'd gathered them all together, waited while they put on their disguises—lifetimes of paranoia didn't die easy—and squeezed them into the twelve-passenger Ford Econoline van he'd borrowed from his *goomba* for just this purpose.

He'd barely left the airport, on 101 North, when the piece of crap van started to cough and shimmy like a TB victim. He pulled off at the nearest freeway exit. It was just a block from a gas station, so he'd told the passengers to wait while he went for help. Nothing wrong with that, was there? At least he didn't have to go far, dressed as he was in an Armani double-breasted pin striped suit, white shirt with lots of starch in the collar the way he liked it, a red tie, and brand new wing-tipped shoes.

He'd had to wait about twenty minutes for the station's mechanic to finish up with one customer, even though he'd tried to slip the guy a C-note to ditch the earlier job. It could have been a lot worse, though. The day before Christmas every housewife, Sunday driver, and certifiable moron who should never be allowed behind the wheel of a moving vehicle got on the road to clog it up and call for help when they couldn't figure out how to get the car out of

"Park." Bah, humbug! When he saw he'd have to wait for the mechanic, he'd tried AAA, but the phone line was so jammed up he was left on hold and couldn't even get through to an operator.

The day had not started out the way he'd expected, to put it mildly.

And it had just gotten worse.

"It's a van!" he yelled at the bored mechanic. "A huge mother! It can't just disappear."

The mechanic leaned against the tow truck and chewed on a toothpick. "Maybe this is the wrong street?" His manner was so lackadaisical, his tone so condescending that Richie was ready to take the toothpick and shove it down his throat.

But then he thought...maybe the jerk-off was right.

Not that he forgot where he left the van, but that his passengers might have gotten it going again and test drove it a little way. Yeah, that was it. Hadn't he heard Joe Zumbaglio used to be called Joey Zoom because he was so good with cars? Although, if it was good at fixing them or at heisting them, Richie couldn't remember.

He rubbed his forehead, then disgusted, flung himself into the truck and directed the mechanic which way to go. Then he directed him another way, and another, until they ended up driving all over the neighborhood, up and down side streets, checking out driveways, back alleys, even along the freeway.

Nothing. No van. No passengers. Only a snickering mechanic.

A small bead of perspiration broke out on Richie's brow. *This isn't happening to me.*

They returned to the gas station and he peeled a fifty off his roll of greenbacks for the driver, the whole time trying to figure out what the hell to do next. He checked the time on the pancake-sized platinum Rolex on his arm. It was a little after one. He had plenty of time. All day, in fact. No reason to panic.

He paced. He'd call a cab, go home and get his car. Yeah, that would work. And while he was at it, he'd make a few phone calls. Just call to say hello, right? And for sure, somebody would say to him, "Hey, Richie, you won't believe what I just saw."

It wasn't as if he could actually tell anyone what had happened, not if he wanted to see Christmas Day. San Francisco Bay was too close by, and he was allergic to concrete overshoes.

Homicide was completely, painstakingly empty. Space-vacuum kind of empty. No telephone rang. No memos to read. Not even an impersonal interoffice e-mail wishing her a "happy winter season."

A little sad, a little lonely, maybe a little sorry for herself for being stuck here at work instead of with her family for Christmas, Rebecca leaned back in her chair and put her feet up on her desk. She'd always wanted to do that. She tapped the eraser end of her pencil against her desk, and watched it bounce. Even the new man in her life, Greg Horning from Vice, had gone back to Cleveland to spend the week with his family.

She sighed. "Jingle Bell Rock" went through her head although she didn't like the song. Then a Snickers bar called her name, and she made her third trip to the candy machine. This time, she was out of change and slid in a dollar bill.

The machine burped, and the bill slithered out again.

She shoved it in; the device up-chucked and spit it back. The junky contraption looked like it was sticking its tongue out at her, daring her to try once more.

She did; same result.

Grabbing the dollar, she returned to Homicide to check her e-mail yet again to see if CSI or anyone else had contacted her. They hadn't.

Not only was Homicide a barren wind tunnel, so was the entire fourth floor of the Hall of Justice. Even the women's bathroom. Heck, she could have used the men's room if she'd wanted. No thank you.

Lieutenant Hollins, head of the division, had given everyone the day off except for Rebecca and her partner. It wasn't that Hollins was being generous; he knew nothing got done on Christmas Eve. Past years, when the staff came in, they fretted about last minute shopping yet unfinished, then went down to the third floor to drown their sorrows with Christmas cheer in the district attorney's office. The punch was so strong, Rebecca was sure the only fruit in it was an orange dipped twice then discarded. Christmas wasn't the time of year a lot of homicides occurred anyway. That was New Year's. All of Homicide would be on duty next week.

She glanced over at her partner's empty desk. Good ol' Bill Never-Take-A-Chance Sutter. He was a snail on the slow road to retirement. With enough time in to collect a pension, he was merely hanging around until he felt "ready" to officially leave. He'd probably show up around ten o'clock today, leave at three or four. Rebecca wondered if he ever would retire. Generally, a person needed something to retire *from*.

Frankly, it didn't matter if Sutter was here or not. Except for the weird death this morning, all was quiet. Too quiet. She tried to rouse someone from the Coroner's office to do the autopsy right away, before they went home or visited the DAs, but so far her calls went unanswered. If no one was willing to do the autopsy today, she'd have to wait until December 26th for the results. Not even the coroner was ghoulish enough to do such a procedure and then go home and carve up a Christmas turkey.

She rifled through the reports of the few eyewitnesses at the mall. Everyone denied seeing or hearing anything. All she could do was wait.

Wait for the fingerprints to run through the system, wait for photos of the victim, wait to use them to scan criminal records for digitized matches. She was tired of waiting, and couldn't help but wonder if the dead Santa had a family who was also waiting—waiting for him to return home.

He looked old, like he could be someone's grandpa. What kind of Christmas would his family have once they learned he was dead?

She'd never forget the first time she had to inform a family on Christmas that the husband and father wasn't coming home again. It was horrible. She shook off the memory. She was a cop; she knew death didn't stop for holy days.

The multi-volume California Penal Code lined the bookshelves behind the secretary's desk in the reception area, kept there both because it was huge and also so it wouldn't get lost in the piles of papers around the inspectors' desks. The way the mall's management had pushed her to shut down the crime scene as quickly as possible had rankled badly. She'd hurried, and didn't believe she'd compromised the investigation by doing so, but she wanted to be able to quote back chapter and verse of the Code if she ever again found herself in a similar situation.

Somehow, she didn't think the managers would have been so bossy if the inspector-in-charge had been one of the guys—Paavo Smith or Luis Calderon, in particular. Nobody told either of them what to do. Then there was Bo Benson, who would have worked out a give-and-take deal, or "Yosh" Yoshiwara, who would have found a way to get what he wanted and had the managers think it was their idea. Bill Sutter would have been a no-show. Only *she* could be pushed around. It was because she was a woman, she was sure—the first and only female homicide inspector in San Francisco.

She'd often been told that she was tough enough for the job. Well, boys, she was about to get even tougher.

Citing the Penal Code was one way to do it.

She sat scouring the complicated index at the empty secretary's desk when a guy she'd never seen before swaggered in. He was a couple of inches shy of six feet, a hundred ninety or so pounds, and about forty years old. His hair was jet black, a little long and wavy on top, and his brown eyes heavy-lidded, down-turned and intense.

She pegged him right away. He was actually fairly good-looking, and could have been appealing, except for one thing. It wasn't the designer threads, the way he carried himself as if he had no fear, or the expensive hardware like the watch that probably cost half her yearly salary. It was those eyes—dark with a certain knowledge and experience—that told her which side of the law this smooth operator walked on. Her instincts twitched and her back stiffened.

"Hey, there," he said. His hands were in his pockets, and he looked over his shoulder a couple of times. "How you doing?" His voice was as mellow and buttery as his brown leather jacket.

"Okay," she said in an even tone. His wasn't the usual greeting for someone coming to this department. "This is Homicide," she pointed out.

"Yeah, I know." He glanced over his shoulder again. "I'm looking for someone. Paavo Smith."

She wondered if it was about a case. The guy looked nervous enough to be about to confess to murder. "Inspector Smith isn't in today. Perhaps I can help you."

He cocked an eyebrow, his gaze definitely rakish. "I'm sure you can, but not in this. I need a cop. What, is he off today or just out on a case? Can you reach him?"

What an a-hole. She stood up to her full five-foot ten-inch height and looked him straight in the eye. "I'm a homicide inspector," she said coolly. "Now, what is it you want, *sir*?"

He took a step back, hands raised as if to fend off a punch. "Whoa, I didn't know death cops came like"—he waved a hand toward her then quickly dropped it—"uh, yeah. Sorry. I just need a little info but, as you said, Paavo's not in today." He stopped; hard eyes studied her, then a half-smile, half-smirk curled his mouth. "Come to think of it, you probably can help. Why not, right?"

"Right." With cool detachment, she returned the look of scrutiny with one of her own and left him in no doubt that she not only found him wanting, but pictured him in an orange coverall. "Follow me."

She headed into the bureau. "With pleasure," he murmured, his voice deep, smooth and definitely sexy. Too bad his personality didn't match it.

o0o

If cops looked like her when he was growing up, he might have been more inclined to like them, Richie thought as he followed the attractive woman into a big, messy room. Rows of desks were hard to see because of all the paperwork piled up around them on bookcases, file cabinets, and computers.

"You read all this stuff?" he asked as she stopped at a desk and motioned him into a folding aluminum chair.

"No. I use it to cut paper dolls." Her chair tilted, swiveled and rolled. She leaned back in it comfortably.

He found himself grinning. So, she had a mouth that went along with the face and body. Not that she was his type. Far from it. To begin with, she was a cop. As they say on TV—*fuhgetaboutit*. Then, she was too tall. If she put on high heels, they'd be like Mutt and Jeff. And he liked women who were soft in all the right places. She didn't look the least bit soft anywhere, yet, she had a body that wouldn't stop. The kind a man could get his hands around, so to speak.

She was older than he thought when he first walked in and saw her with one side of her straight blond hair tucked behind an ear, the other side draped down half covering her face as she poured over some thick books. When she looked up at him, her light touch with make-up added to the youthfulness. Her face was shaped like a triangle with widely set smoky-blue eyes and prominent cheekbones tapering down to a small, pointed chin. Most women he knew would give their eyeteeth for a bone structure and big eyes like hers. He was surprised she didn't doll up a little more—her white blouse, black slacks, and black boots with low one-inch heels looked like a uniform. But then he reminded himself that she was a death cop. Why bother to wow the corpses, right?

Although he felt a lot more alive just looking at her.

She opened a spiral notebook. "Name?" she asked, reaching for the green pen at the corner of the desk.

He gripped the cold metal arms of the chair and shifted, trying to find a comfortable way to sit in the hard seat. "Richard Amalfi."

"Amalfi?" She stilled, a sudden question in her blue eyes. "You're related to Paavo's fiancée?"

"Yeah. Angie's a cousin."

"I see." She shut the notebook. "What can I do for you, Mr. Amalfi?"

"You can call me Richie,"—he glanced at the nameplate on her desk—"Rebecca."

"You can call me Inspector Mayfield." She twisted the top back onto the pen.

"Yes, ma'am, Inspector Mayfield, ma'am."

She regarded him like a schoolteacher with a truant.

His voice rumbled over the quiet room. "Look, I need you to help me find some, uh, friends. They're older...gentlemen." He wracked his brain, trying to figure out how to best explain this. "They're in a van. Here's the license number." He pulled a piece of paper from his pocket and gave it to her.

"You want me to find this van?" she asked.

"Well...yeah," he replied, palms upturned, open. "Why else would I be here? Call somebody and then tell me where it is. I got to go pick up the guys. They shouldn't be driving around this city all alone. It's a dangerous place, you know."

Her eyes narrowed. "How long has the van been missing?"

He slid back his sleeve and looked at his watch. "Two goddamn hours." He ran his knuckles against his jaw as thoughts struck of what the guys could have done in that time.

"Two hours? That's not very long." She slid the paper with the license number to the corner of her desk. "I'm sure they'll turn up. They're probably sight-seeing or something."

"I called everybody I know." His loud voice echoed through the empty office. "Nobody said nothing about them showing up. This morning, I picked them up at the airport, and I'm supposed to see that they get someplace special this evening. That's all. But now, they're gone. And today's important."

"Because it's Christmas Eve?"

That's as good a reason as any. "Yeah, right. And it's up to me," he exclaimed, hands pressed to his chest, "to get them there." *Enough of this!* His impatience was about to boil over. He lowered his voice. "Look, Inspector, it's twelve old guys in a big Econoline." He leaned over her desk, picked up the license number and slapped it in front of her. "Call around. Maybe somebody's seen them."

She tapped the paper against the desktop. "Nobody's going to notice such a thing."

"They might."

"Why should they?"

He clamped his mouth tight. He really hadn't wanted to say, but she was right. There was no reason anyone would notice just any twelve old geezers. That wasn't the case here, though. He supposed he was going to have to tell her, much as he didn't want to. He would have told Paavo, but he trusted Paavo. Paavo was a man; he understood stuff. He didn't know if this skirt would. She acted kind of uptight, come to think of it. "Maybe I can reach Paavo at Angie's," he said, standing.

"And how is he going to help you?" She kept folding and unfolding the license number and seemed almost amused by his predicament. He was getting more pissed off by the second. She added, "Paavo's off duty."

He sat again. She was right, damn it. He looked back over his shoulder—an old habit, and one that gave him time to think. "Just a few phone calls to some dispatchers or something," he said. "Just to ask them if they've seen the van. That's all I need, and I'll take it from there."

She seemed to think for a minute, then nodded. He figured she wasn't exactly rolling in cases. "Okay. If that's what you want. I can make a few calls, but you're just wasting your time and mine. Nobody's going to have noticed."

"Well...there's more to it," he admitted.

She waited.

He swallowed. "The twelve old guys I mentioned"—she nodded—"they're all dressed up like Santa Claus."

If anyone had told Rebecca Mayfield this morning that she'd end up in a black Porsche sitting next to a guy who looked and sounded like he stepped out of a bad remake of *Pulp Fiction,* she would have told him he was nuts. If he went on to say that she'd be investigating a Santa Claus corpse who looked flat as a mosquito on a car windshield and was now in hot pursuit of a van with twelve more jolly ol' Saint Nicholases, she'd have called the men in white coats for him.

She glanced at Richie Amalfi, who had just swung to the wrong side of the street to pass a cable car, nearly causing a head-on with a Gallo Wine truck, and suppressed the urge to stomp on the brake pedal—with his foot on it—

and write him up.

Earlier, she phoned the dispatcher at Central Station and learned, to her amazement, that a report had come in from Chinatown about a van filled with Santa Clauses blocking the area around Waverly Place and causing a commotion. Waverly was a narrow side street parallel to Grant Avenue in the heart of Chinatown, and lined with tongs—legitimate family associations, or so they told the police. The dispatcher had just sent two squad cars to get the old guys out of there before the scene erupted into another tong war.

"Sounds like your boys are in Chinatown," Rebecca said to Richie when she got off the phone.

"Holy Christ!" Richie got up and headed for the door. "Thanks."

Mrs. Mayfield hadn't raised a stupid daughter. Some guy dressed in red pajamas had gone splat on her watch, and now twelve more were careening through the city with Lucky Luciano, here, in hot pursuit. There had to be some connection. No way would she believe it was a coincidence.

"Wait up!" She grabbed her purse, jacket, and was clipping her hair into a barrette at the nape of her neck as she followed him. "I'm going with you."

"No, you aren't." He spun on his heel in the doorway, hand on the frame as if to physically block her way.

"Yes, I am," she said, nose to nose with him as she put on the jacket. "You don't know where in Chinatown they are."

"It's a huge van. How hard will it be to find it?"

Her jaw jutted as she smiled. "You'll never know, will you?"

His eyes narrowed. "Why do you want to get involved in this?"

"Civic duty?" she suggested. "Helping the elderly? I mean *you*, not the Santa boys."

"Me?" He grinned and dropped his arm. "All right, Inspector. Have it your way."

They had another argument when they reached the parking lot. She didn't like getting into cars with strangers, although him being Angie's cousin helped. He absolutely refused to ride in the rickety city-issue Ford Taurus and leave his car in the lot. Her choice was either to ride in the Porsche or to follow it—and then have to deal with parking, losing him in traffic, or having him simply take off and the Taurus be unable to keep up.

No argument. She folded her long body into the sleek little sports car, and was filled with suspicion over where and how he'd gotten it. The powerful motor hummed and darted into traffic.

"So," she said, assessing the cable-car passing, wine-truck menacing maniac at the wheel, "you picked up twelve old guys at the airport. Are they all friends?"

He sped up at the yellow light, hit the intersection as it turned red and cruised across. "Something like that, yeah."

"You're obviously worried about them. They might get lost, I suppose."

"They know the city."

"No need to worry, then," she offered, closely watching his reaction.

His mouth wrinkled, but he didn't answer.

"What about their families?" she pressed. "Have you notified them?"

"Look, Inspector, cut the third degree. They're missing, all right? It's Christmas Eve. There's people they want to be with. Although"—brown eyes darted her way—"maybe you don't know about that kind of stuff. Why are you working today?"

She never answered personal questions from suspects. Not that he was one. Yet. "Tell me what you were doing with the old guys. It might help us find them."

"No family here, huh?" he persisted.

"My family's in Idaho, thank you. Now, if you expect me to help you, I need some information."

"They're going to ring bells for the Salvation Army." At her sneer, he added, "I volunteered to drop them off at their pot-stands."

An eyebrow lifted. "So you're one of Santa's little helpers."

"Well..." He screeched to a halt behind a car who'd stopped for a pedestrian. "Just like you said. Civic duty." He lowered the window, stuck his head out and yelled, "Move it, douchebag!"

Okay, she told herself, *so he's not going to tell me what he's up to.* She hadn't exactly expected he would. His furtiveness told her that it was probably shady and likely to end up with someone dead. Someone like her victim this morning.

She directed him toward Waverly Place. Half a block before reaching it, the traffic stopped completely. A crowd of people surrounded the entrance to Waverly.

Richie threw the car into reverse and was just about to careen backwards when another car pulled up behind him. And right behind it was a Coca-Cola truck. "What the—!" He pounded the steering wheel.

The streets of Chinatown were narrow, often one-way, and cluttered with double-parked cars and trucks unloading food, souvenirs and tourists. The streets around Waverly were clogged under normal circumstances, and Waverly itself was even worse. Richie couldn't go backwards, forwards, or down the sidewalk.

He shut off the motor, yanked out his key, jumped from the car and ran toward Waverly.

"Hey!" Rebecca climbed out and watched his retreating figure. What the hell, she thought, and took off after him. If someone stole or towed the Porsche, it was his problem, not hers. She mentally ticked off his fifth traffic violation in as many minutes: illegal parking.

Richie marched up and down the small street, puffing and snorting. "I don't see any van," he yelled. "Why don't I see the van?" He furiously kicked a bag of refuse, knocking it over. Its loose ties fell off, and rotting contents spewed onto the sidewalk. She eyed it, then him in distaste. Public littering.

"The report," she began, "said they went into a mahjongg parlor next to the Hop Sing Tong—"

Before she finished, Richie took off down the block. "There it is." He pointed toward a dark brown brick doorway. It was non-descript except for some Chinese writing painted on the side. She eyed it skeptically. "Don't tell me you read Chinese."

"No. Just the words"—he pointed at two characters—"mah and jongg."

With a calm swagger, Richie went inside. She'd never been in one of the Chinese gaming parlors before. They were illegal as hell, but the cops were under strict orders from the city fathers to leave them alone. You could either chalk it up to "understanding diversity" or "bribes." Take your pick. She followed.

The room was shrouded in a thick haze of smoke. Considering all the gambling going on, the city's no-smoking policy was a non-factor. A jumble of tables with fluorescent lights over them filled the room. People sat, four to a table, looking almost like a bunch of bridge players except for the intensity of the their expressions. Even now, in late afternoon, the room was nearly full. The clinking of game tiles was deafening. No one paid attention to the newcomers.

Richie strolled up to a pudgy bald-headed Chinese man at the desk and the two greeted each other like long lost pals. They talked quietly a while before the man shook his head and pointed up the street.

"They split," Richie said, ushering her toward the door. "He thought they were going to a restaurant, or trying to shake the cops who were looking for them....Though, uh, they'd have no reason to be wary of cops," he quickly added. "None at all."

"Why were they here?" she asked, knowing better than to expect an answer. She gave the mahjongg tables one last look, then let him steer her out.

They reached the street just in time to see a large white van go by on the opposite end of Waverly Place, over on Washington Street. The van must have been double-parked or have done something people didn't like because a crowd of elderly Chinese men shook their fists and yelled after it in Cantonese. No translation needed.

"God damn!" Richie ran to Washington and watched the van lurch uphill. So did he. Rebecca sprinted up the hill with relative ease, and was surprised that he managed to stay in front of her.

The van turned at the corner onto Stockton, and by the time they reached the intersection, it was nowhere in sight. Richie bent over, hands on knees, trying to catch his breath, his face a brilliant shade of purple.

They returned to his car to find that the crowd had dispersed and his Porsche was now the only thing blocking traffic. The Coca-Cola and Toyota drivers stuck behind him had apparently decided to push it out of the way. One man tried to break into the car with a slim jim lockout tool while the other stood at the back of it, ready to push. Richie lifted the guy away from the car window, grabbed the lapels of his jacket, and tossed him onto the street.

The man looked up at the outraged Richie, apparently decided he had no complaints, and scrambled back to his beat-up Camry. The Coca-Cola driver followed.

Rebecca scowled at all three. Assault and battery on Richie's part, and possibly destruction of property depending on what happened to the Porsche once the two geniuses got it rolling. She was tempted to arrest them all, then go back to Homicide and use a more traditional approach to crime solving.

"You coming?" Richie asked as he got in. She hesitated, but Richie might be her only lead to the dead Santa for a long while. She jumped into the passenger seat and before she'd even shut the door, he stomped on the gas pedal.

"Why did the Santas go to the mahjongg parlor?" she asked and fastened her seat belt.

"Is that a joke?" He zigzagged past obstructions to proceed around the block. "Like, why did the chicken cross the road?"

"Ho, ho, ho." Her fingers itched to smack him. Hard. "What did they want in there?"

"They went for old time's sake, I guess," was his unsatisfactory response. For a man who emoted big time, he was remarkably tight-lipped, which meant he had secrets.

The Porsche disappeared into the Stockton Street tunnel, the easiest route between Chinatown and the downtown area, and popped out near Union Square.

As opposed to Chinatown, which always resembled a corner of Hong Kong in the 1950's no matter what the season, holiday or time of year, the Square was lit with Christmas decorations. Up ahead was Macy's, to the right Saks Fifth Avenue. On the opposite street, the St. Francis Hotel, one of the city's oldest and finest, took up the entire block. Smaller exclusive shops and boutiques ringed the Square and nearby Maiden Lane. Rebecca couldn't afford a handkerchief in one of the Lane's shops, as opposed to Angie Amalfi and—by the looks of him—her insane cousin.

Here, people rushed about doing last minute Christmas shopping. She'd gotten all hers finished two weeks before Thanksgiving. That was when stores held truly big sales, and there were no crowds. She could shop quickly, efficiently, and save money besides. Same with wrapping the presents and sending them to her parents, her brother and his wife, and her two nephews back in Idaho. By shopping early, she could ship them in the most practical manner as well. No need to waste money on overnight or even on priority.

Her Christmas season was efficient. No hubbub; no crowds teeming with energy. None of this kind of holiday excitement filling the air and making her spine tingle.

"Damn! Look at all these people." Richie broke into her thoughts as he waited impatiently three cars back from a red light. "I still have four presents to get. Looks like I'll be short."

"The disadvantages of your profession, I suppose." Her tone was thick with sarcasm.

Something flashed across his dark eyes. "My profession? You don't know beans about my profession. Maybe you should look at your own." A laughing, package-laden couple jaywalked in front of them. He turned almost rueful and surprised her by saying, "Not exactly normal jobs for normal people, are they?"

Maybe it was the holiday bustle, maybe it was the sudden glint of honesty she imagined had been in his eyes, maybe it was the fact that they were both alone and working on Christmas Eve, but she said quietly, "Then we wouldn't be who we are, right?"

"Right." His elbow rested on the doorframe, hand to chin, and speaking more to himself than her in a voice so soft his words were almost imperceptible said, "How bad that would be?"

She glanced at him, but made no response. He met her gaze. The Porsche suddenly seemed a lot smaller, and he seemed a lot closer. She turned her head, and for a long moment they sat in awkward, mutual silence, spectators to a festive, holiday scene, outsiders together.

The mood was broken when Rebecca spotted a large white van turning into the underground parking garage beneath Union Square. "Is that it?" she asked.

"We got them now!" Richie punched the air as he swerved out of his lane, crossed oncoming traffic and cut in front of cars lined up waiting to enter the garage. A burly driver honked long and loud, then got out of his car and stomped toward them. Rebecca rolled down the window and held up her police badge. He backed off.

Richie roared up and down narrow parking lanes until he spotted the van. Every nook and cranny nearby was filled, often illegally, and he had to park an entire floor away. "Let's stay close to the lot." He headed for the elevator. "They should come back soon. You married?"

The question surprised her. "No," she replied, and focused back on the problem at hand. "Why not just wait near the van?"

"Hell, no." Thick concrete pillars held up the ceiling. Above was a park with trees, grass, and winter plantings. "I'll wait 'til I'm dead to have dirt and people walking around on top of me. Besides, I don't do underground in earthquake country. Engaged?"

"No." Not that it was any business of his, she thought. He was like a bulldog. "Don't you know the chance of there being an earthquake while we're waiting down here is practically zero?"

The elevator bell bonged and the doors opened. "Yeah? Well tell that to the people who died going across the Bay Bridge during the last big one. I'm going up to the Square. I'll take my chances above ground."

"But you could be trapped in an elevator," she reasoned, stepping on.

"It's faster than taking the stairs." His hands twitched, his whole body bounced with nervous energy.

"What about tall buildings?" She wasn't sure if she was intrigued or simply enjoyed making him squirm. "Do you go up in them?"

"I would, if I had business up in one." When the elevator doors opened, he catapulted off it then tugged at his jacket in a show of casual indifference. It didn't fool her. "Let's walk around the park." He forged ahead without waiting, obviously ill at ease with her questions. Behind his back, she smiled.

The area was crawling with Santa Clauses. Everywhere they looked one or two stood, collecting money or handing out fliers. A violinist played "I'm Dreaming of a White Christmas." Rebecca usually could take or leave the song, but for some reason—perhaps because she was so alone this year—the song reminded her of Christmases past, in

189

Idaho, surrounded by family, and enjoying the snow-covered beauty of the land.

Her eyes grew misty. She felt Richie's gaze on her and tried to hide her feelings. She didn't like that this man, practically a stranger, seemed to read her so well. The only man she wanted to understand her was engaged to another woman and probably spending a warm and joyous Christmas Eve with his fiancée.

How ironic was it that she was with that woman's scoundrel of a cousin?

They were soon out of range of the violinist and neared a children's choir singing about city sidewalks dressed in holiday style. Suddenly, she was glad she was out of Homicide and here, surrounded by the warmth of the holiday—even if she was with a whack job a few trucks short of a convoy and searching for old coots who sounded like Santa's elves on speed.

"There they are!" Richie grabbed her hand and pointed toward the big, main entrance to Macy's a block away. "Come on!"

He plunged into the street, pulling her with him, jaywalking between cars and busses. She was glad the traffic was all but stopped due to the crowds. She couldn't believe he'd spotted the Santas. She could scarcely make them out in the chaos, and she'd been trained in crowd surveillance.

He ran up to them. Only about eight were there. "Where's the rest of the boys?" he asked.

The Santas faced him. They weren't the guys he was looking for. "Are you kidding me?" Richie's face went through a series of contortions: anger, disbelief, mulishness. He reached out and tugged at one of the Santa's beards. The elastic stretched and revealed a frowning mouth. "Uh...sorry." Richie let go and the beard snapped back into place. A Santa, bigger and more muscular than the others, stepped up to Richie, then held out a Salvation Army kettle. Richie donated, and then hurried away.

"It was a good try," Rebecca said.

"Yeah." He smoothed his shirt then the jacket, and ran his palm, diamond-pinky ring flashing, against the sides of his hair to smooth it. The whole time his back was to the Bible-toting Santas as if he couldn't care less about them.

They walked down to Market Street, heads swiveling from side to side, up, down, even under a time or two. "I've never seen so many goddamned Santa Clauses in my goddamned life!" Richie exclaimed. The streets swarmed with jaunty red caps and white beards mixed among the throngs of shoppers.

Rebecca spotted a group of Santa hats marching toward the Ferry Building. "Are your Santas short?" she asked.

"Yeah! Where?" He looked where she pointed, then frowned. "What the hell. It's worth a try."

They hurried after the group, but slowed down as they neared. The Santas all carried Girl Scout cookies.

Richie kicked a mailbox, making a dent in it, and uttered a string of Italian curses. She ignored him, except to tick another violation: mutilating Federal property. "This is dumb," he complained. "Let's get back to the van and wait."

"Why don't you tell me why you want to find the Santas?" she asked.

"Why don't you tell me why you care?" He shot back.

"Hey, you asked for help." She sidestepped the question.

"Yeah? You're supposed to be investigating murders," he pointed out. "Nobody's dead. Just some old guys missing, yet you've glommed on like Crazy Glue. It don't fit, Inspector."

She wasn't ready to tell him about her dead Santa. Not with the way he'd been behaving.

They were in the parking elevator before she said, "Tell me why you need to find the Santas, and I'll tell you why I'm interested."

He glared at her and they existed in a vacuum of sullen silence, a silence that thickened appallingly when they got off the elevator.

The van was gone.

"Where to now, boys?" Joe Zubaglio, otherwise known as Joey Zoom, asked as he slowly drove the van up and down the city streets. Skinny, with sagging cheeks and gnarled hands, he was seventy-five and the only one who still had a valid California driver's license—so to speak. In case they got stopped, they didn't want to take any chances. The driver's license gave his name as Hiram Bernstein.

"I think we should'a stayed downtown." Lorenzo the Slug scratched his fake beard. He used to be called the Slug because he was so good with his fists—a slugger. Now, though, it was because he had to stop at a bathroom every thirty minutes so it took him forever, slug-like, to get from one place to another. That was also why the others let him ride shotgun next to Joey Zoom. He could get in and out of the van easily and no one had to sit next to him if they didn't find a john in time. Nobody told Lorenzo that, though. They let him think he was the same strong pugilist as ever. That was the thing about the crazy names the guys gave each other, they were for fun, honor, and at times, a surprising amount of affection.

"Three women handed me money," Lorenzo continued, his brows thick with tangled white strands. "I was just standin' there, too. Wish I'da known how easy it was to make a buck wearin' a Santa suit. Woulda saved me a lotta trouble."

"What? You gotta pot 'a rubble?" Frankie Vines shouted. "What you gonna do wit' rubble?" Frankie didn't have a nickname. They tried to call him Frankie the Ear because of his obvious difficulties, but he thought they said Frankie the Beer and went on a toot that lasted three years.

As usual, everyone ignored him.

"How was we supposed to know everything's changed so much?" Lorenzo asked. "Who woulda thought Big Leo retired? I was countin' on him to help!"

"I told you I heard he died," Peewee Carducci whined in a high voice. He had a long narrow face and oversized ears that jutted out like wings under his Santa hat. "Just like today. I told you we shoulda used a wood chipper. That's the way we did it in the old days."

"Naw, Big Leo didn't die," Lorenzo said confidently, his scrawny Santa suit-clad chest puffed out. "We'll find him and get him to help. He knows everything, and if he don't wanna help, we'll make sure he remembers who he's dealing with."

"He don't remember nothing if he's dead," Peewee muttered.

"Who's Fred?" Frankie shouted.

"Maybe he's got alkaselzer," Guido the Cucumber piped up. He was called that because of his love for antipasti, but he liked to brag that it was for another reason. Guido was round with a big belly, a jowly face and thick ankles that seemed to ooze over his shoes. "You know, that memory thing. Like Ronald Reagan."

"Yeah, and maybe he thinks he's president, too," Joey Zoom remarked with a sneer. "Time's wasting. We gotta find him and take care of business. After, maybe we'll call Richie. Who's got his number?"

All were silent, but then two of the Santas were asleep, four had turned off their hearing aids, and two were too busy looking out the window to pay any attention to the conversation.

"Well, somebody's gotta have it," Joey Zoom muttered.

"At least we got ridda him," the Cucumber said, tugging on the Santa suit around his thick thighs where the material was cutting into his circulation. "And Joey Zoom still has his stuff." He high-fived the Santa next to him so hard that poor old Joe fell off the seat. Six of the Santas were named Joe, which made things confusing sometime.

"Try North Beach," the Slug said. "That's where all the *paisans* hang out. And I gotta use a bathroom. Somebody there'll know how to find Big Leo." Everyone agreed.

As they drove by St. Francis of Assisi, they saw an elderly woman dressed in black step out of the church. She appeared confused, as if she wasn't sure which way to go.

Joey Zoom slowed way down, concerned about her, when two young men walked by. One of them grabbed her purse. She hung on tight and fell to the ground, but he yanked it hard and ran off with his buddy.

The van roared to life. Joey bore down on the thieves.

They angled right and so did the van. Pedestrians jumped out of the way; city trash bins flew. The young men turned down a narrow side street only to discover it dead-ended. High- pitched girly screams mixed with the squeal of brakes. The van stopped just in time. Six more inches and the assailants would have been spending Christmas in purgatory.

Lorenzo jumped out, snatched the purse from the dumbfounded muggers who stared blearily at the van of Santas.

"Don't mess with little old ladies," Lorenzo ordered as Joey backed the van out of the alley. "Or, with Santa Claus."

As Richie drove in circles, speeding, swerving and swearing, around the downtown and Mission Street areas, Rebecca wondered once more if her guess that her dead Santa was connected to the missing Santas wasn't a bad mistake. Maybe she had had a sudden glucose attack from her failure to get a Snickers. Maybe she'd let the lure of figuring out just what Richie Amalfi was up to, seduce her. Not, of course, that she would ever want to be seduced by Richie Amalfi!

She glanced at his dark, dangerous looks. Definitely not her type at all...although, he did kind of remind her of Al Pacino in his younger days. She drew in her breath.

But if, as he'd said, there really were twelve Santas out there, why? What were they planning? She'd seen enough of Richie Amalfi to believe that any plan he was involved in had nothing to do with holiday giving.

Holiday taking was a better possibility. And now, it was up to her to prevent it. Whatever "it" was. She needed a different approach. One to lull him.

"Do you spend Christmas with Angie and her family?" she asked casually.

His eyebrows jiggled with surprise before he said, "Naw. My mother cooks. We eat. Watch a little football.

Tell old family stories. I'll take home a plate of food that'll see me through the next couple of days." His gaze slid her way. "You?"

"I'm on call over the next thirty-six hours. So, I'll spend the day tomorrow basically hoping nobody gets killed. I won't see my family until January."

"What's—"

His question was cut off by the ringing of her cell phone. It was Traffic, calling with an answer to her earlier query.

She listened, then hung up and studied Richie. It was time for answers. Her voice turned hard. "Who do you know at the Stonestown mall?"

His face registered confusion. "Nobody. Why you asking about the mall?"

"There was an accident—an auto accident—near the airport this morning."

"Yeah?"

"You picked your friends up at the airport."

"So?" He waited, and when she said nothing he swung the car into a red zone and shut off the engine. She braced herself for another explosion of temper, ready to meet it head on. Instead, he shifted in his seat to face her, his voice low, and somehow even more deadly. "You think just because I lost some old guys I'm responsible for everything that goes wrong in this town?" He sounded almost indignant. "What's with you, lady? Why are you here anyway? You can get the hell out of this car and go back to Homicide. It's not as if I'd miss your help."

She weighed her options. It'd be in the newspapers soon anyway, so it wasn't exactly a state secret. "All right," she said. "Today, around eleven, a car went off an overpass by the airport. It landed upside down and was pretty much flattened. By the time the cops and paramedics got there, though, the driver's body was gone. An hour later, a man dressed in a Santa suit was found at the mall. He was dead. His injuries made it look as if he'd fallen from a great height."

"A Santa suit?" Richie seemed dumbfounded by the story, but at the same time, his eyes darted. "What do you mean? Like he fell or jumped out of a building?"

"Maybe. The problem was, he was in the middle of the parking lot. There was nothing near he could have fallen from."

Richie blinked. "So...it's sort of like he fell out of—"

"Yeah," she said quickly, not wanting to hear the words she knew he was thinking.

Richie chuckled.

"It's not funny!" Rebecca stated for the umpteenth time that day.

Something about her indignation made his chuckle develop into a belly laugh. "You're wrong, Inspector. It is funny. Maybe you should do blood work and give Santa a posthumous DUI." But then he glanced at her frown and his humor died. "Okay, so what does it have to do with me? You were at a mall, for cryin' out loud. They're lousy with Santas."

He was right—it should have made sense, but it didn't. "He wasn't wearing a mall-issued suit, for one thing. Wasn't recognized, had no I.D., and nobody seems to be missing any Santas but you. Are you sure you were expecting twelve Santas and not thirteen? Or maybe you only had eleven, and the dead guy is the twelfth?"

He looked startled at first, tense, then fell suspiciously quiet. "When I left the airport, I had twelve Santas," he replied, but then he asked, "What does he look like?"

"He's older, late sixties, seventies. Gray hair. A small guy. The photographer has probably e-mailed me copies of the best digital photos from the scene by now. If we go back to Homicide I can show you. Maybe you'll recognize him."

"I got a better idea." He reached behind the seat and pulled out an iPad. He turned it on, punched a few buttons, then held it toward her.

"Log onto your network," he said.

She shook her head. "Won't work. It's a closed, internal system, lots of security."

"Trust me."

Dubious, she took the device and did as told. In a matter of seconds, even faster than her supposedly secure terminal at work, she was into the system. She didn't want to think about it.

The photographer's photos were there. She flipped through them, then put the clearest one on the screen. "Are you squeamish about looking at dead bodies?" she asked.

"You talking to me?" Richie reached for the photo, glanced at it and blanched. Before he turned white then an anemic green, she saw recognition in his face. He handed the iPad back to her. "Never saw the guy before."

"You're lying."

"I never lie." He cranked the ignition and pointed at the computer. "Keep it close. Let's get going."

"Where to?"

"I don't know. It's a small city, a big van. Something's got to show up."

"You're lying again!" Any minute now, she was going to pull her Beretta on him, no doubt about it. "You've got someplace in mind. Now, tell me where we're going."

Richie ran long fingers through blue-black hair that flopped in waves when he was through, almost but not quite thick enough to hide the thinning spot at the back of his head. She noticed a hint of gray at the temples, a slight cragginess to the skin, and lines at the outer corners of his eyes. Normally, she liked such signs of maturity in a man. She might need to rethink that.

Richie's next comment brought her back to earth. "I said I didn't recognize the guy in the photo. But I know someone who might."

The building was shaped like a triangle. The pointed nose, on the corner of Columbus Avenue, held the front door. In the early days of the last century, LaRocca's Corner was one of the most popular mob hangouts. These days, it was mostly filled with yuppies who liked the post-Prohibition décor, and wiseguy wannabes. Rebecca never doubted, however, that a few of the real thing continued to frequent it as well.

Richie's mouth scrunched as he perused Rebecca head to toe. "I better go in alone. You wait."

She said firmly, "No."

"They'll wonder who you are. What you're doing with me."

"Tell them I'm a friend."

He tugged an earlobe, and looked uncomfortable. "Well..."

She glanced down at her black jacket, slacks, boots, and white shirt blouse buttoned to the collar. She'd pulled her hair back in a barrette as they'd left Homicide. He was right. She didn't look like someone a guy like him would hang around with. Which was, frankly, not a bad thing.

"Just wait a minute." She dug some lipstick out of her purse and put it on, then unfastened the barrette and shook her hair loose. Taking off the jacket, she cinched her belt tight, then rolled the sleeves of her blouse to the elbows and unbuttoned the top two...no, the top three...buttons and spread the collar wide.

"Now?" She expected the scrunched-mouth look again. Instead, she noticed his Adam's apple move as if he swallowed hard as his gaze slowly drifted down her long frame, and then back up again. He reached up and gently pushed a couple of strands of hair back from her eye. To her surprise, his expression softened as he gazed at her. Then he nodded. For some reason, her breathing sped up a bit.

They walked inside with his arm around her waist. He kept her close as they approached the bar, waving to people, calling out greetings in Italian and English, and using the kinds of nicknames she thought had been made up for shows like *The Sopranos.*

He ordered bourbon and water and quietly asked her what she wanted. She hesitated a fraction of a second then said, "Gin and tonic."

The understanding in his eyes was even more unsettling than the fact that she had ordered alcohol on duty. Well, she could order it, but it didn't mean she had to drink it.

As he talked to the bartender and others, she pretended to sip her drink, listening carefully, even though little of what they said made sense. Most of it was almost in code, and sounded suspiciously like the kinds of conversations one might have with a bookie. The only difference was that this time of year they talked football, not horses. Christmas and college bowl games seemed to go better than mistletoe and holly in this little establishment.

A very drunk man staggered over and put his arm around Richie. "How's it goin' pal?" he slurred.

"Fine, Pinky. Looks like you've got a heat on. You got cab fare to get home?"

"Naw. I'm not ready to go home anyway." He eyed Rebecca suspiciously. "Say, where's Sheila?"

"She's home with the kids. Let's get you a cab."

"No need, Richie, really."

Richie sweet-talked him to the door.

Home with the kids. Interesting, she hadn't thought of Richie as being married. He didn't seem settled, and hadn't mentioned a wife and kids earlier when he talked about Christmas at his mother's. He might be divorced, but then, a lot of these hoodlum types didn't talk about their wives. The women kept the house, raised the kids, prayed in church for the ever-deteriorating souls of their husbands, but nothing more.

Given all she'd seen so far, it was interesting that Richie Amalfi was on Angie's father's side of the family. From what Paavo told her, Sal Amalfi was straight—a businessman who'd made millions on shoe stores and real estate. Angie's mother's relatives were another story. One branch of Serefina's family, headed by her uncle Bruno Bacala, also called Bruno the Tweeds because of his stylish clothes, was connected up to the armpits.

Richie tapped her arm. "You got the gizmo in your purse with the picture of the dead body?"

She handed it over and he showed the bartender.

"Sure I know him," the man said. "It's Cockeyed Lanigan. Mean old coot."

"He's dead," Richie stated.

"No fooling? Man, the old guys are dropping like flies. Nobody's going to mourn Lanigan, though, you can count on that."

"Any idea why he'd be headed to the airport this morning?"

"Not me. The only guy who ever talked much to him was Leo Respighi. Maybe he knows."

Richie's attention was distracted from the bartender when a new customer came in laughing about some old Santas who broke up a mugging. The kids they caught not only gave up the old lady's purse, but went into the church to thank God they were still alive.

The clientele at LaRocca's Corner laughed as if it was the funniest thing they'd ever heard.

Richie was all over the newcomer finding out just where the van was, who was in it, and where it was going. The information didn't help much, but at least they knew the Santas were in the neighborhood.

By the time they left LaRocca's, it was fairly dark out, even though it was only five o'clock. "Damn!" Richie said, scowling at the sky. "It's going to be harder than ever to find them." He checked his watch. "I've only got four hours."

"Then what?" Rebecca asked. "Your Santas turn into a pumpkin?"

His mouth wrinkled into a worried frown. "No, I do."

Just then, right before their eyes, a big white Econoline van drove by on Columbus Avenue, then turned onto Mason.

"Holy shit!" Richie cried and took off after it.

The van started up a hill. Richie and Rebecca tried to catch it but were losing ground when a cable car clanged for them to get out of the way. As it went by Rebecca grabbed the pillar that went from the back guardrail to the roof. She used it to pull herself onto the bottom step on the cable car's side.

Richie was behind Rebecca and couldn't grab the same rail. Instead, he lunged for the back of the car. Both hands grabbed the top of the guardrail. He had to run faster than she thought possible to keep his footing, and then he shot up, lifting a foot onto the bottom rail and pulling the second foot up after it. Fortunately, the soles of his shoes were rubber so he didn't slide right off again. That surprised her; she'd expected he'd be the type of guy who always wore slick leather. He held on tight. "Watch out!" he shouted.

She looked up to see the back end of a UPS van jutting out into traffic, only a half-foot from the side of the cable car. She gasped. He grabbed her shoulder and swung her toward him just in time to avoid having her face—and every other part of her body—decorate the truck.

He was still holding her tight when a red-faced conductor stormed out of the cabin. "What the hell is wrong with you two idiots? You want to commit suicide you do it on somebody else's car! Now get up inside and pay like everyone else, or get the hell off!"

The cable car was halfway to the next corner when it had to stop behind a row of cars for a red light. Richie saw that the van was stopped as well.

Ignoring the conductor, he leaped off the car and ran toward the van. When Rebecca saw what he was up to, she followed, but not before mouthing "Sorry," to the outraged ticket-taker.

Violation: riding public transportation without paying fare.

"Open up!" Richie yelled, grabbing the driver's door handle and pounding on the window. "What's the matter with you guys?"

Rebecca was on the passenger side, yanking on the doors, but all were locked. She looked inside, and sure enough, just as Richie had promised, there were rows of little old Santa Clauses, dark brown eyes gaping back at her in surprise and wonder. She had to admit that until that very moment, a part of her simply hadn't wanted to believe his story was true.

She was tugging on the door handle with both hands, one foot on the frame for leverage, when the light turned green. Other cars began to move. She yelled, ordering the Santas to open up. Suddenly, the door swung open and slammed hard against her. The window hit her nose, hurtling her end over end. Black lights and bright stars exploded in her head. Luckily, she rolled in the direction of the sidewalk out of the way of the oncoming cars. The van rocketed away.

Richie's hands tucked under her armpits and lifted, helping her move onto the curb where they both sat. "You okay?" He took out a handkerchief—she didn't think anyone used them any more—and pressed it to her nose. Maybe in his line of business he needed one. When he lifted it away, she saw blood. There was no maybe about it.

The world turned as red as her blood. She'd been dragged all over town, had a drink in a bar with a nest of criminals, broke enough laws to spend a week in jail, and now she'd been hit in the nose by a van of Santas. Her breath started coming short and fast; her ears rang; everything began to tilt.

Suddenly, he grabbed the back of her head, shoved it between her knees and held it down. Her hand found his chest and she strong-armed him, then sprang back up. "What the hell are you doing?" she shrieked.

"You turned pale," he said. "You gotta take it easy."

"Take it *easy*?" Her temples pounded. "How can I take it easy around you! You moron! You dolt! You—" She grabbed the handkerchief from him as she felt blood trickling down her nose to her upper lip and covered both. "You pithant!" She lisped.

"Calm down," he ordered as if talking to a child. "You're hurt."

"I'll show you hurt!" She swung her arm and socked him in the ear, hard, then jumped to her feet.

"Ow!" He rubbed the side of his head.

"I must be crathier than you are to have wasted my time on you and your bullthit!" The thought that she was no closer to knowing why he was driving around with the Santas, what he was up to, how it was all connected to her dead guy, and the fact that she was lisping, turned her purple with rage. She lifted the handkerchief long enough for choice words to tell him exactly what she thought of his goofy ideas, his friends, and his heritage.

A car driving by stopped and a middle-aged man gawked at her, his mouth hanging open. "What's your problem?" she demanded. He sped away.

She spun back to Richie, still sitting on the curb watching her in stunned silence.

Abruptly, she stopped, stared down at him, then lifted her head and walked away, once again holding the handkerchief to her nose.

He shook his head in wonder, then got up and followed.

The twelve Santas marched single file into LaRocca's Corner wishing Merry Christmas to one and all. Half followed Lorenzo the Slug in a rush to the bathroom, while the others took over two tables, three barstools, and ordered twelve Boiler Makers. Earlier, they'd had lunch at the replacement for the Old Spaghetti Factory, and espresso at the replacement for the Café Trieste. Neither, they'd concurred, was as good as the "real" places they remembered.

Once they got settled, after a few words with the bartender about the Good Ol' Days, Guido the Cucumber said, "By the way, we're looking for Big Leo Respighi. Seems he's given up mahjongg. Even closed his business. What's up? You know where we can find him?"

The bartender looked surprised. "Leo? I hadn't heard he'd closed up shop. I suspect he's home with the old lady."

"No way," Guido said. "His wife's dead."

Stricken, the bartender put down the rag he'd been wiping glasses with. "Anna Maria?"

"Hell, no!" Guido scowled. "That's Punk Leo's wife—"

"Don't call him Punk if you know what's good for you," the bartender warned.

"Who cares?" Guido said. "We're talking his father—*Big* Leo."

"Hey, fellows, I'm sorry," the bartender said. "Leo's old man died about six, seven years ago."

The other Santas were listening and they all doffed their caps in memory of Dead Leo.

"See, I told you!" Peewee muttered. "Maybe we shoulda thrown that guy offa pier this morning. It mighta been safer."

"Who's gonna appear? Morley Safer?" Frankie Vines shouted his questions, then looked at all the bowed heads. "Jeez, did he die, too?"

"Frankie, shuddup," Joey Zoom warned.

"We gotta plan." Lorenzo the Slug sat at a table and

the Santas gathered around him. "I thought Big Leo would be the one to help us. He knew a lotta things money can't buy. We needed him, and now..."

"Poor Leo," the Cucumber muttered.

"I got an idea," Joe Pistolini, called Joe the Pistol for obvious reasons, said. "I know a woman who'll help us. Her uncle's a good friend."

"I hope so," the Cucumber said. "I'm starting to get a little tired with all this eating and drinking and gabbing. I gotta save my energy for tonight."

The others wearily concurred.

Richie was trying to figure out if he should get rid of the woman beside him. He had to admit, for some weird reason he liked having her there, but she had no part in this, and it could end up being dangerous for her.

Somebody was pulling a fast one here, and he was in the middle of it. What if the extra Santa had shown up at the airport and said he was supposed to be part of the group? Richie wondered if he'd have believed him and let him join the others. Or better yet—what if he'd bumped off one of the real passengers and took his place? Would the others have known he didn't belong? In fact, what if one of them already *was* a fake? What if they'd all been kidnapped? How would he explain how he'd let *that* happen on his watch?

The thought turned him ashen.

Some insider had to have leaked out the information about the Santa costumes. Who was the snitch, and whose side was he on? Were the old boys, right now, in danger?

He doubted it. They hadn't looked the least bit scared when they tried to sucker punch him with the van's door.

He'd chuckled about the Santa costumes when they'd first been proposed. These old geezers were only "somebodies" in their own minds, he'd thought. Some had served time. Others were lucky, had never been caught, and the statute of limitations had long passed on anything they might have done.

On the other hand, considering that they were on the lam and another Santa was dead, maybe they'd been right to be paranoid.

He thought about letting someone on the inside know what was happening, but doing so meant he had to admit that he'd lost the twelve guys. Twelve! Who in the hell loses twelve men? That was more than a frigging football team!

It was embarrassing. Not to mention potentially deadly. Scratch the "potentially." Much as he hated to admit it, the inspector was his last, best hope.

The chance of the Santas being picked up by the cops was high. Frankly, he never imagined they could drive around in a van all day and not get nailed. None of them could drive a straight line, he was sure, and he doubted they could keep this up for very long now that it was dark out. Half the guys had cataracts and the other half were legally blind. No way could they continue night driving without running into something.

Once that happened, Rebecca would get the call from the dispatcher, and he'd rush with her to wherever they were, pick up the pieces and deliver them on time.

"Your nose stop bleeding?" he asked.

"Yes." She'd put the handkerchief in her purse. She'd clean and mail it to him.

"Good. Doesn't look like you'll have a shiner for Christmas, either." He tried not to chuckle, but failed.

"Yeah, well..." The way she'd lost her temper irritated

her. Paavo Smith would never have done anything so undignified, and she shouldn't have either. She needed to put things back on an even keel. "Your kids must be excited about Christmas," she said. "Are any young enough to still believe in Santa Claus?"

He jumped. It wasn't the kind of question a guy liked to hear. "My *what*?"

"Kids. The ones you talked about at LaRocca's."

"I don't have any kids! None that I'll admit to, anyway," he added. An old joke. He was sure he didn't have any, though he'd lived pretty wild in his younger days.

He glanced at Rebecca. She was a quiet woman, but he liked it when she talked to him, even if she said some oddball stuff. "What made you think I had kids?"

She looked confused. "Somebody asked about Sheila, and you said your wife was home with the kids."

"Wife? No way! She's an old girlfriend. A widow. She's got kids. May her husband rest in peace, but after I dated her awhile, I could see why he decided to check out so young. I don't have nothing to do with her anymore. Or...not much."

"No wife, no girlfriend?" she asked.

"No wife. Lots of girlfriends," he said with a grin. "None serious. You?"

She thought about Greg Horning at home in Cleveland for Christmas. "Could be," she admitted. "I'll see how it works out after the holidays."

He nodded. "Another cop?"

"Sure. Who else do most cops date?" she asked with a rueful shrug. "We're the only ones who understand us."

"That's what I figured," he said. "I warned my cousin Angie about that, but the Amalfis are all pretty stubborn."

Her eyebrows lifted. She couldn't imagine anyone

having a negative thought about Paavo Smith. He was the best cop she'd ever met. Angie Amalfi, on the other hand... "That's funny, because all of Homicide warned Paavo about Angie."

He did a double take. "You crazy? Angie's a great catch."

Rebecca frowned. "A lot of women go for the uniform."

"Paavo's plain clothes." Richie eyed her. "Why? Who do you think is better suited for him?"

She stared straight ahead. "I have no idea."

He eyed her firm mouth, her small pointed chin, jutting proudly. "Oh, yeah?" he asked.

She glared as if she'd gladly see him burst into flame. "That's what I said."

He drove with no more questions, and stopped at a house half way up Telegraph Hill on Vallejo Street. "Wait here." He got out of his Porsche.

To his irritation, she simply got out of the car. Before he could open his mouth, she said coldly, "If you think I'm about to twiddle my thumbs in your car while I've got a dead body to investigate, you're wrong. If this guy knows anything, I'm going to hear it."

Although his ear was still smarting from the smack she gave him, he stuck his face in hers until they were almost nose-to-nose. "He won't talk to a cop," he shouted, arms spread straight out at his sides.

"He'll talk if I take him in," she pointed out.

She was going to get him bloody well killed! "For what reason? Because I said he might know something? No. He'll say I was wrong. Look, Inspector, I need to find my twelve guys. If they know something about your dead merry old elf, you'll find out, but only after I've got them. So, back off!"

"Go to hell," she said calmly.

"Trust me," he pleaded, running out of ideas and time.

"Not on your life."

He glared. "Then keep your trap shut and don't— whatever you do—let on that you're the law."

She glared right back. "I'm not making any promises."

He grumbled and swore, but grudgingly led the way up the outside stairs to the front doors. There were three of them, in the typical style of San Francisco flats. He rang a bell and one of the doors buzzed open. Inside a narrow foyer they faced another long flight of stairs.

"Hey, *goomba*—it's me, Richie."

"Richie! *Caro mio!*" a woman's voice called down. As they reached a bend in the stairs, they looked up to see a middle-aged woman with a square face and short, black curly hair standing at the landing. She wore an apron and was wiping her hands, a diamond and platinum ring on each finger, then held them out to give Richie a big hug. He hugged her in return.

She stepped back and eyed Rebecca. "Who's this? A new girlfriend, Richie? She's very pretty."

He took Rebecca's hand and pulled her forward. "This is, uh, Becky May...Mason. Becky, meet Anna Maria Respighi." Anna Maria grabbed her hands and welcomed her. "Is Leo here?" Richie asked.

"He's in the back, watching TV. I'll go get him. Sit down in the kitchen. You hungry, Richie?" She patted his face. "You and your girlfriend, you want to eat something?"

"No, sweetheart," he said. "We're fine. Just got to talk to Leo."

"*Aspetti.* You come to my house, you eat." She gave them both a glass of red wine and made up plates of the leftover rigatoni and meatloaf still on the counter from dinner. While she zapped them in the microwave, she lit herself a cigarette and asked Richie in Italian all about his new girlfriend. He only prayed Rebecca didn't understand as he sang her praises in the bedroom and the kitchen—the only places he figured that mattered. He decided she didn't have a clue what he was saying since she neither blushed or shot him with the gun he knew she was packing in that big black purse she lugged around everywhere. Come to think of it, she probably never blushed.

With the cigarette smoldering in an ashtray, Anna Maria put a plate in front of Richie, and another before Rebecca. "*Mangia,*" she said, then softly to Rebecca. "I hope you like it."

She said it so sweetly, Rebecca found herself murmuring, "I'm sure I will." The smell of the spicy red sauce and the hint of garlic, onion and oregano in the warming meatloaf, reminded her that she was starving. The food was delicious.

Richie, too, ate with gusto. "You're looking too skinny, Richie," Anna Maria said.

"I'm not skinny—just not so heavy anymore. I was letting myself go. The hell with that. I joined the gym. Run, box. It's good for me. I actually feel better."

"You were overweight?" Rebecca asked between bites.

"For a little while," he murmured, then stuck his head further down toward his plate.

"A woman," Anna Maria called to Rebecca as she stood by the open back door for the last few drags. "She was no good. He's lucky to be rid of her."

"Thanks, Anna Maria," he said, washing down a swallow with wine. "That's just what I came here to listen to you talk about. Where's Leo?"

Rebecca found this conversation interesting, however.

"Was that Sheila?" she asked Anna Maria.

"Sheila? No, no, no. It was Jeannie. She was—"

"Enough already!" Richie shouted.

Anna Maria laughed, crushed the cigarette butt, and headed down the hall to find her husband.

Rebecca's eyebrows were still high on her forehead. "A lot of girlfriends, huh?"

He shrugged.

She was going to take up the gauntlet when a big man walked into the kitchen wearing a satin robe patterned with Christmas trees and reindeer on a red background. Richie and Rebecca stopped eating.

Punk Leo's bare legs looked like toothpicks below the robe, and his feet were shod in loose, floppy black patent leather slippers. "'Ey, Richie, how's it going?" His deep voice reverberated throughout the kitchen like a boom box.

Leo sat down at the table. Richie introduced Leo and Rebecca, calling her his "acquaintance." Leo's brows slanted downward as he nodded. Leo's nose, lips and ears were all oversized and blubbery. The only things small were his eyes and, it seemed, his intelligence.

"We're trying to find out who this guy is." Richie pretended not to know Cockeyed Lanigan as he showed Punk Leo the thirteenth Santa's photo on the small computer screen.

Leo no sooner looked at it then he threw it onto the table and bellowed, "I don't know him, and I don't want to know him."

"What do you mean?"

"He's trouble. I don't have nothing to do with him. Nothing. Is that clear?"

"He's dead, Leo," Richie said starkly.

Leo's face darkened. "Dead? You show a picture of a

dead guy to me? You do that in my house! Bring me seven years bad luck!" He lunged, toppling Richie and his chair to the floor.

Anna Maria screamed. Using his arms and legs, Richie was trying to shove the big man off him. Rebecca avoided where she looked as the two scrambled on the floor and the bathrobe lifted, revealing more of Leo than she'd ever wanted to see.

Rebecca made one attempt to separate the men and got an elbow buried in the stomach for her troubles, doubling her over to gasp for air. The gun she had in her purse tempted her, but it would give away that she was a cop, and Richie had warned her not to. She could use some of the karate she'd learned, but she didn't like the idea of breaking anyone's bones on Christmas Eve.

Anna Maria solved her dilemma by grabbing a dust mop and shoving and shaking the head of it between the two men, bopping first Leo then Richie in the face. Clouds of dust billowed with each smack. When the two men started coughing, she swung the mop even more forcefully, hitting their noses and foreheads, then chest and shoulders. With each swing, more dust flew, making them pant more, which meant they had to take bigger and bigger gulps of air and only managed to get even more dust in their mouths.

Finally, they let go of each other and rolled to their sides, eyes watering and choking.

Cold-cocked by a dust mop. Rebecca tried not to laugh, but as she looked at Richie gasping from his exertions, the thought struck that she was actually having fun, and that she hadn't been around such an interesting and provocative man in a long, long time. God! Where had that come from? The crack on her nose must have been harder than she'd thought.

"Cover yourself, Leo!" Anna Maria yelled. "What's wrong with you two? It's Christmas Eve! You should be ashamed!"

As Anna Maria helped Leo struggle off the floor, Rebecca held out a hand to Richie.

"You get that filth out of my house!" Leo roared, facing Richie again. "I don't know Cockeyed Lanigan and I don't give a damn that he's dead!"

"Do you know what he was up to this morning?" Richie asked, stubborn as usual.

Leo went beefy red. "What are you, some kind of cop? I don't know nothing! Get the hell out of here, Richie," he said.

"And if you know what's good for you, you'll go home and forget about all this."

"The cops will find out what happened, Leo," Richie said, wearing a predatory, lopsided grin. "After all, the guy's dead."

"Yeah?" Leo adjusted his robe. "Then that means there really is a Santa Claus."

The Santas were standing outside the Fior d'Italia restaurant waiting to meet the woman Joe the Pistol had phoned. To their surprise, as they cheerfully wished Christmas greetings to passers-by, people kept handing them money.

They took it.

Then, a little boy and girl went walking by. The boy looked about seven and the girl six. They stopped, glared at the Santas and stuck out their tongues.

As they started to walk away, Guido the Cucumber

limped after them. "What's the matter with you kids?" he yelled. "Don't you know better than to treat Santa Claus that way?"

"We hate Santa," the boy said.

"Yeah, we hate you," the girl chimed, but her blue eyes filled with tears.

"Hey, what's wrong? Santa didn't do nothing to you," Guido protested.

"You aren't coming to our house," the boy said. "Daddy's sick and can't work. We wanted bikes, but Daddy said no way. Santa doesn't give things like that to poor kids. Seems to me, the rich kids could get their parents to pay for things, it's the poor ones Santa should help."

The Cucumber nodded. "Well, your Daddy may be right most of the time, but there's twelve of us Santas here, and maybe we can work something out. You tell me where you live, so I won't have trouble finding the right house, and maybe between the twelve of us, we'll be able to help you."

The kids looked wary. "I thought Santa Claus knows where everybody lives," the boy said.

"Well, yeah, but look at us, we're getting old. You know old people are forgetful sometimes."

The kids gave their address, and all the Santas wished them Merry Christmas as they left.

"What we gonna do?" one of the Joes asked.

"Think guys. Who do we know who can help?" Guido looked from one to the other.

"Santa's dead," Peewee said remorsefully. "We know all about it."

"Where's Santa's bed?" Frankie Vines shouted. "I'm ready to lay down. All this is a lotta work!"

They ignored him, as usual.

"No problem. I know someone," Joe the Pistol said with a big smile. "We were just talking about his old man, too. Punk Leo—he's sells toys and all kinds of stuff. I'm going to his house tomorrow for Christmas dinner. We can call him."

Joey Zoom stared at him, annoyed. "Did you tell him we was all coming here today? We weren't supposed to tell no one."

"What's the big deal? He's expecting me," the Pistol argued. "His wife's aunt's husband was my wife's brother-in-law, God rest his soul, so we're related. I told Leo not to worry, that we was all dressed in Santa costumes so nobody'd recognize us."

"I hope you're right," Guido said, "and I hope he knows enough to keep his mouth shut."

"Sure he does. Let's go find a pay phone. I'll call him. You'll see. Punk Leo's a nice guy, despite what everybody says about him. He'll get some bikes and deliver them. No problem."

"Hey, wait a minute," Lorenzo the Slug said, his bushy eyebrows knitted with suspicion. He'd come in late to the conversation since he was using the snazzy facilities at Fior d'Italia. "If you talked to Punk Leo, how come you didn't know Big Leo's dead?"

Joe the Pistol shrugged. "I ain't talked to Big Leo since the summer of eighty-three. We had a fight. I was gonna ask Punk Leo about him when we got together. Don't need to now."

"What was the fight about?" Lorenzo asked.

Joe looked remorseful. "Damned if I can remember."

"You were talking about Stonestown," Richie said after

a long silent period punctuated only by curses as more time elapsed without a van sighting. It was nearly seven-thirty. "I remember that Leo runs an import-export business. Furniture, toys, all kinds of stuff. I think his warehouse is in Stonestown."

Rebecca's head snapped toward him. "That means he probably ships furniture around the country, or the world..."

"Exactly," Richie said.

The more Rebecca thought about it, the more sense it made. Wrap the body up good, pack it in a furniture crate, put on a sticker to Madagascar, and then pay a few bribes once it arrives. Who'd know? Or, even simpler, ship it to Las Vegas and pay some friends down there to create another lump out in the desert far from town. Easy. But, *why?*

And, if someone were trying to get Cockeyed Lanigan's body to Leo's shop, what if they freaked out at all the security around the mall due to Christmas, dumped the body and took off?

"Let's go check the place out," she said.

"Why?" Richie looked at her as if she'd lost her mind. "My guys won't be at Leo's business."

"How do you know?" she retorted. "He acted more than a little suspicious. He clearly knows more than he's saying."

There was more under-the-breath muttering about women and cops. "All right, Inspector. We'll take a quick look, then we're out of there and back to North Beach. I've got the feeling they aren't far away."

Stonestown was almost completely deserted since it closed early on Christmas Eve. They found Leo's import-export business, then drove to the loading dock area in back of the building. All the lights were out. It looked quiet and empty.

Richie parked along the side of the building, then they tried the doors, hoping to find one open and something going on in the warehouse. They didn't.

"Well, it was worth a try," Richie said, dejected. "I should give this up. I don't know where else to look, what else to do. I guess it's time for me to face the music."

"Which means what? Are you in trouble? We've spent the whole day searching, Richie, and I don't even know why."

For a moment, the way he gazed at her, she thought he might open up. He didn't. "You don't want to know. Trust me. I'm supposed to deliver them somewhere. That's all there is to it."

They started to walk back to his car. "Well, maybe they'll go there on their own," she consoled.

"They don't know where it is. It's a secret." He glanced over his shoulder a moment. "I'm sure they expect someone will help them, but I can't if I don't know where they are."

"That makes no sense," she insisted.

"It doesn't, except that they're old guys who are used to others looking out for them."

"As in, they've been in jail most of their lives?" Rebecca asked suspiciously.

"As in...you might be right about that. Whatever it means, I lost them, and I'll have to pay the consequences."

"You make it sound as if the consequences are dangerous." They parted and he walked toward the driver's side, she to the passenger's.

He looked upward. The stars shone brightly in the clear night sky, the moon just rising over the mountains.

"I'll find out," he said.

He was maddening. It was like talking to a cipher. "Well, you might be wise to worry." She faced him over the top of the car. "A killer is out there somewhere. Maybe he's hunting down your Santas—maybe not. But he's there, and if you're involved, you could be in danger as well."

"Me? I never do anything dangerous. I'm allergic to it."

Just then a shot rang out. Richie ducked after feeling the bullet whistle by his head. Rebecca dropped behind the Porsche. A dumpster was behind her and she ran to it, curled between the trash bin and the wall, waving for Richie to follow. He did.

As far as she knew, Richie Amalfi wasn't armed. But she was. She slid the gun from the special pocket in her handbag where it was held down with a Velcro strap. She thumbed the safety off and waited. One more shot, and she'd see where the shooter was hiding.

"Cover me," he whispered.

"They only do that in movies," she hissed and made a grab for him.

She was too late. He sprinted off in the direction of the shooter and stood behind a telephone pole. Another building was beside the import-export loading dock, and that one also had a large parking area with pillars and ramps. Richie headed for it.

With a curse, she followed. Spotting a smashed beer can, she grabbed and tossed the can far as she could toward her right, hoping the sound as it landed would draw fire and she'd be able to spot the gunman.

It didn't.

She scrambled after Richie. She had no idea where he'd disappeared to, only that he needed some protection...and she needed to catch a killer.

She heard a "thump" then an "Oomph!" followed by another "whack, thump, blam." Quickly, she followed the sounds. Two men held Richie while Leo pummeled him.

She stretched out her arms, a two-handed grip on her gun. "Stop right now, Leo!" she shouted loud to make herself heard over the swearing, punching, and Richie's grunts of pain. "I don't miss when I shoot!"

Leo's arm was high when he looked over and saw the barrel of a powerful Beretta facing him. It wasn't some wimpy twenty-two. It was a cop's gun—city issue.

The two guys with him decided to show respect for a serious firearm. They let go of Richie and ran. She let them go. It was Leo she was after.

"So, your girlfriend's a cop," he said, his voice sneering as he faced Richie who was sitting on the ground rubbing his ribs and stomach. "What were you thinking bringing a cop to my house? Here, to my business? I told you to keep away from me, but you wouldn't listen! This isn't over, Richie."

"Yes, it is," Rebecca said, showing her badge. "I'm bringing you in for questioning about the death of..."—she hesitated, but it was the only name she knew—"Cockeyed Lanigan. You're not under arrest yet, but you come quietly or you'll be charged with assault and battery."

"I didn't hurt Lanigan! I was trying to stop him from..." Suddenly, he shut his mouth. "I know nothing. I want to talk to my lawyer. I won't answer any more questions."

She knew enough about the law and lawyers to know there was no way she was going to be allowed to interrogate Leo on Christmas Eve after he'd asked for a lawyer. Probably not Christmas Day, either. She didn't have enough probable cause to go after an arrest warrant.

Not yet, anyway. "You'll have plenty of chance for that," she said. Let him stew awhile, she thought, as she turned her attention on Richie. "Are you all right? Do you want to go to a hospital?"

"I don't need a hospital." He touched his bleeding, swollen lip. "I just need my handkerchief back. And I want Leo to tell me where the old Santas are." He faced Leo. "I know you know about them."

"Sure," Leo said eying the two. "I just got a couple of kid's bikes for them. That's why I'm out here and saw you two sneaking around my warehouse. Why?" Slowly the light seemed to dawn. "Is that what this is about? You're trying to find them? You're the transport, right? And you lost them." He chuckled. "I was wondering about that. Well, I'll be damned!"

"Where are they?" Richie demanded again.

Leo folded his arms. "No way, Richie. You ruin my Christmas, I'll ruin yours."

"Damn you!" Richie moved forward.

Rebecca put an arm out, stopping him.

"Eat me," Leo said with a nasty smirk.

"Cool it, you two." Rebecca put her gun in the handbag and handed Richie the handkerchief, then faced Leo. "Why did you shoot at us? Why beat up Richie?"

He looked disgusted. "The first was to scare you away, the second was to show what happens to somebody too stupid to run after being shot at. Officially, however, I thought he was burglar."

Rebecca had to admit to a certain logic to that. "I'll let you go tonight, but stay close to home and to your phone. We can talk tomorrow—"

"But it's Christmas!"

"At eleven in the morning. Have your attorney call

me." She knew the guy would call and say he and Leo wouldn't be there, but it was okay. Leo wasn't going anywhere, and her gut feeling told her he wasn't a murderer.

Stupid and crooked, yes. Murderer, no.

"What is it they call you?" she asked, directing her question at her so-so suspect. "Punk Leo? Makes sense to me. Get out of here now."

He ran to his car, casting aspersions on Richie's manhood the entire way.

Angie Amalfi looked at the clock when she heard the knock on her apartment door. It was early for Paavo and besides, the knock was too quiet for him. He had a cop's "open up or else" knock, even when coming to see her. They were going to go to dinner and then to her parents' house for Christmas Eve.

Angie was a petite woman with wavy brown hair streaked with light auburn highlights. She'd been looking forward to this Christmas Eve for some time—the first one for her and Paavo as an engaged couple.

She opened the door, then her mouth dropped and she stared. Was this a joke? Her mother, Serefina Amalfi, stood in front of her dressed up like a vision of a very w-i-i-d-e sugar plum wearing a Christmasy red dress decorated with large white polka dots, her black coat haphazardly tossed over one arm. Springs of mistletoe formed a corsage. Serefina's cheeks were fiery red. She'd obviously been testing the eggnog.

That wasn't the whole story, though. Behind her were more little old Santa Clauses than Angie had ever seen. "What's going on, Mamma?" she asked, wide-eyed. "Did you raid the North Pole?"

"These are my good friends," Serefina's words slurred as she linked arms with two of them. Her coat fell and Angie picked it up. "We've been celebrating, talking about the good old days. And we have a favor to ask of you."

"Where's Papà?" she asked, sticking her head out the door to better see through the blaze of red.

Just then, her neighbor Stan Bonnette, probably because of all the commotion, opened his apartment door, gazed into the hall at the plethora of Christmas spirit, gawked, and then quickly shut the door again. His dead bolt clicked into place.

"Your papà is home," Serefina answered. "He's waiting for us, the old fart. He doesn't like to go out, as you know." She lowered her voice to a stage whisper. "And he doesn't approve of all my friends." She put a finger in front of her mouth and said, "Shush."

"Mamma, I think you need some coffee," Angie said, pulling her inside.

"Your father is such an old man!" Serefina wailed. "Not like *miei amici!*" To Angie, her mother's friends looked eighty at youngest. "So, are you going to make them stand in the hallway, or are you going to help us?"

Angie instinctively put her arms up to block the door. It was Christmas Eve and Paavo was coming over soon for their private celebration. This couldn't be happening. With brows creased, she asked suspiciously, "Help you with what, Mamma?"

After Richie's lip stopped bleeding, he looked at his watch. It was after eight. "Damn! I've got to get going."

"Drop me off at Homicide?" she asked.

"Sure."

They rode in silence except for the time he asked her what she was looking for in her purse. She told him it was her key card to get into Homicide after hours. Actually, it was one half of a homing device that she planned to stick under the Porsche's passenger seat. The other half remained in her purse. She wasn't about to let him ride off, possibly to meet with the killer she was looking for, without doing anything about it. She could tell from the way he drove, constantly checking side and rearview mirrors, that he was far too paranoid about being followed for her to tail him the normal way.

The magnet on the homer make a little "dink" as it met the metal bars under the seat and she coughed, trying to cover the sound. He glanced her way. She patted her chest. "Sorry."

"Look, Inspector," he said, "I'm sorry about this, too. The day didn't go quite the way I'd planned. I didn't mean to put you in danger. Or myself."

"I know. For me, it goes with the territory."

He stopped just outside the Hall of Justice parking lot. Her car, a five-year old Jeep Cherokee with four-wheel drive, a V8 engine, and a CD player, perfect for when she went up to the mountains or to some remote beach for vacation, was the only one left in the center of the lot. A couple of security guard cars were right next to the building.

"Looks like everyone's gone home for Christmas Eve," she said.

"Yeah. Guess so," he murmured, facing her, his gaze intense. "Look, uh..."

She practically jumped out of the Porsche. "See you around, Richie Amalfi."

Understanding eyes caught hers, held a moment, then he nodded. "Okay. You, too, Inspector."

She shut the door, and he drove off.

Hurrying to her car, she set up her half of the homing device on the dashboard. It whirred for a moment, not doing a thing, then began a steady, pulsating beep. Success!

She started out, heading left as she'd seen him go. She'd ridden with others as they'd used one of these devices to follow a suspect, but she'd never done it on her own and it was trickier than she'd imagined. Richie would turn a corner, and she'd go straight, only to realize her mistake when the beeps grew weak and slow. It'd be a matter of U-turning when possible, if not racing madly around a block to pick up the strong steady pulse once again.

They headed up Twin Peaks and were nearly to the top when the beeps grew fast and loud. She slowed to a crawl and when she rounded a curve in the winding road, she saw the Porsche in a driveway, Richie getting out.

She stopped and shut off the car's lights then backed up onto the side of the road. The streetlight illuminated him as he walked to the front door and unlocked it. She wondered why he wanted to go home. Again, doubts about everything he'd told her that day surfaced.

The lights turned on, one by one, as he went through his house. The place looked like the kind of home he might have. Modern and redwood, with a bow-shaped plate glass window in the front giving him what she imagined must be a sweeping view of the city. She waited, fairly certain he wouldn't be staying home alone all evening. She'd follow in hopes that wherever he went, she'd learn about the twelve Santas, her dead Santa, and perhaps what this day really had been about.

Twenty minutes later, the inside lights started to go off. Richie appeared in a clean suit—his other was wrinkled and filthy from all that had happened to him that day. He got back into the Porsche.

She ducked down in her SUV and waited until he was well out of sight and the homing device began its slow beeps that told her it was safe to follow.

Presidio Heights was an area filled with mansions of the rich and famous, including politicians and some of the top medical specialists and lawyers in the country. She expected to go straight through it when the beeps began to grow faster and faster. He must have stopped, she thought. She pulled over. This was one of the few parts of the city with street parking readily available. It was because there were few apartment dwellers vying for space, and many of the mansions had added underground parking to keep their expensive cars safe from the elements and thieves. For a moment, she could scarcely believe she was in San Francisco.

She got out of the SUV. At the corner she stopped. Ahead was a brightly lit mansion with many cars parked near it, Richie's Porsche among them.

She phoned dispatch to find out who lived in the house. To her surprise, the answer wasn't readily available. A major search had to be performed before she got a name: Giorgio Boiardi.

"My God," she muttered. The name was familiar. Back in her SUV she turned on her Blackberry handheld with its wireless Internet and prayed it would work in this area. It had cost her an arm and a leg, but was handy for her job.

It connected. Within seconds, Google verified her memory and added to it. Giorgio Boiardi, mobster, headed

West Coast operation 1949-1978, in prison 1979-1992 when released due to old age and infirmity.

Curious, she searched for his birth date, and when she found it, looked again to make sure she was reading it right. He was born exactly ninety years ago. Today was his birthday.

This must be a birthday party. And all the old men...could they all have been...?

She had to swallow hard. Had she stumbled upon a group of old criminals gathering in one place to celebrate his birthday with the *capo di tutti capi?* The Don? Is that what was happening?

No wonder Richie wouldn't tell her what was going on. How many of the guys he was looking for had outstanding warrants? How many could she pull in to finally serve time for the crimes they'd committed? That was the reason for the Santa suits. Not that they were a bunch of do-gooders, but because they were wanted men! They needed to hide their faces. What better way than as Santa Claus the day before Christmas?

And Richie Amalfi was in the middle of it all. The big softie was trying to help old men—old *crooked* men—to have one more birthday and Christmas celebration together. She shook her head at the thought.

Now what? One person who was a cop and yet understood the Amalfis came to mind—Paavo Smith. They needed to talk. She tried his cell phone, but it went straight to messaging.

Intuition sparked and she flipped through the stored addresses on her cell phone.

A cheerful, feminine voice answered the call. A few minutes of conversation yielded more than she ever imagined.

She put the light beacon on top of her car, turned on the siren, and sped across the city. The city was tiny, but between traffic jams and traffic lights, it could easily take a half hour to go a few miles. Fortunately, the streets were pretty empty.

Most people were home with their families, not racing around hoping to make a career-establishing, big time arrest.

She left her SUV by a fire hydrant, and nearby was the white Econoline. She all but rubbed her hands in glee. She was on the right track after all.

Impatiently, she waited for the elevator to bring her up to the top floor of the building. She'd never been there before, but she'd heard talk about it often enough to know not only how to find it but exactly what it would look like inside.

The door opened. Angelina Amalfi looked prettier than ever in a red silk dress with matching shoes and gold and pearl jewelry. Rebecca had never even owned dyed-to-match shoes. She felt frumpy as she realized what her once white blouse and crisp black slacks must look like after today's exertions. And she'd never even put the barrette back in her hair. She buttoned her jacket, hoping that might help.

"Come in," Angie said. "We've got eggnog and lots of cookies. The last batch of biscotti is still baking—and Paavo's back from the grocery now, too. We used a lot of sugar tonight."

Rebecca's gaze swept over the apartment before settling on that of her fellow inspector. The living room was much more attractive than she'd expected. The furniture was a mixture of antique and modern. She'd imagined it would be gaudy with dark wood and Victorian curlicues as far as the eye could see. Instead, it was light and peaceful, much simpler and more tasteful than she'd thought...or, than she'd hoped.

Paavo was standing in the dining area talking to a heavy-set older woman. He excused himself and approached, a drink in one hand, the sleeves on his white shirt rolled back, his tie slightly loosened, and with a smidgeon of flour on his brown slacks. He looked relaxed and...happy. Not the stern, serious man he always was at work. Her heart contracted.

"What's the problem, Rebecca?" he asked, knowing she wasn't there on a social call. "I heard you were looking for me."

Earlier, when she'd called simply to ask for Paavo to talk over all she'd learned with him, she could hardly believe what Angie told her. Now, she had a duty to perform.

Santas sat around the dining room table, on the petit-point sofa, antique Hepplewhite chair, and across the room on a pair of wingbacks. A couple of them stood in the kitchen. They still wore their suits, but their hats and beards were off. Even sitting, she could tell that most of them were little men. Perhaps once large and forceful, they now looked stooped and frail. They were *old*.

"I...um..." She looked from one Santa to the other. Canes were everywhere. At least no one used a walker. Hauling them all into jail was going to be a bit more awkward than she'd imagined. What would the AARP say about this? "I've got to question them, one by one."

"That'll take some time," Paavo said. "They're planning to go somewhere for Christmas Eve, although I get the feeling none of them know how to get there."

"None of them are suspects," she said, "but someone

might know something." She faced the group and asked for their attention, then introduced herself. "Cockeyed Lanigan was killed this morning, and I'm trying to find out if anyone here can help in my investigation of his death."

"Cockeyed just died?" Joey Zoom said, surprised. "I thought he was already dead."

"I told you! People ought to use the wood chipper, like in the good ol' days!" Peewee exclaimed.

Joe the Pistol turned to Serefina. "If I'da known you was so chummy with all these cops, I never woulda called you!"

The others told him to shush.

Rebecca knew what was going on: they'd spent a lifetime conditioned not to talk to a cop. "I know where you're supposed to be tonight," she said. "And I can take you there, but not until I learn something about Cockeyed Lanigan."

As one, they all started to put on their beards and hats.

"I don't know why I'm bothering with this get-up," Lorenzo muttered. "We're already at a goddamned cop convention."

"Hold it, everyone," Paavo said. "Rebecca's okay. She just needs answers to a few questions."

"Easy for you to say," the Cucumber sneered.

"Wait! He's my son-in-law to be," Serefina protested. "You trust me, you trust Paavo."

"We trust Paavo. Just not *her*." Joey Zoom waved his thumb at Rebecca. "She comes here threatening. The hell with that!"

Rebecca realized the folly of her completely wrong approach with these men. "Look, I've just got a couple of questions."

"Tell the girl," Serefina urged. "Nobody liked

Cockeyed."

The Santas eyed each other.

Finally, Joey Zoom spoke. "Cockeyed was bad. Word was, he, uh, hated a Big Somebody. Real big. Maybe he wanted to get that somebody. Thought he could follow us around, find out where the party was, and then sneak in wearing a Santa suit. Now, I ain't saying that's what happened, but it could be."

The others nodded.

Rebecca didn't buy it. "So Cockeyed was going to somehow use you guys to get to this Big Somebody, but then he just happened to get himself killed?"

The Santas all shifted nervously. "Look, we saw Cockeyed following us at the airport," Lorenzo said. "Joey Zoom took care of the van so we'd get rid of Richie, but when he pulled off the freeway, Cockeyed tried to follow. I think he made a mistake and went off the overpass instead."

At Rebecca's questioning expression, Joey the Pistol added, "Cockeyed wasn't called that for nothing. He musta got rattled, and did a swan dive."

The others agreed, some loudly.

Rebecca and Paavo traded glances. "If Cockeyed's death was an accident," she said, "how did he end up at Stonestown Mall?"

The Santas all turned expectedly to Joey Zoom. "As I see it" he said, "Punk Leo spilled the beans to Cockeyed, and then realized that if Cockeyed hurt Big Somebody, Leo'd be toast. So, he followed Cockeyed to try to stop him. He musta seen when poor Cockeyed was called by His Maker. Maybe it scared him, who knows, and he didn't want to leave the body where there might be questions about him and his Santa suit. Word gets out, you know, and Big Somebody—he's good at puttin' two and two together."

At Rebecca's nod, Joey Zoom continued. "Punk Leo probably figured out a way to get ridda the body. But with all the security guards at the mall, he got cold feet and stuffed the body someplace hoping to get it later. But he didn't hide it so good, and it got found."

"Isn't that sweet?" Serefina said, clasping her hands to her ample breasts. "Punk Leo saved the D—, I mean, Big Somebody from Cockeyed and only disturbed the accident scene because he wanted to help. *Madonna mia*, what a dear boy!"

Twelve Santa heads bobbed up and down in agreement.

Paavo looked at Rebecca and shrugged as if to say, "Could be." He was right, she thought. Punk Leo did a lot he shouldn't have, but murder probably wasn't included. Still, it'd be up to the D.A. and Leo's lawyers to sort it all out.

As for the old Santas, she probably could haul them into City Jail on some pretext—reckless driving, if nothing else—and see if any outstanding warrants turned up.

Her eyes strayed to the beautiful Christmas tree in one corner of the living room; her mind replayed the scene of Richie and her in Union Square earlier that day, watching the shoppers and tourists, listening to Christmas carols....

And something loosened in her heart. She looked at Paavo who was regarding her steadily, with trust, and then at Serefina's anxious face.

"One more question," she said to the group. "One thing I didn't understand. Since Richie Amalfi was your driver, why did you run off and leave him?"

"Why not?" Lorenzo the Slug wrinkled his mouth in

disgust. "He was a pain in the ass, thinking he had to baby us, watch out for us, tell us to do this, do that. We've taken care of ourselves for eighty years and don't need some young punk doing it now! Besides, we wanted to get a present for a dear friend who's celebrating his birthday today. Something that money can't buy, and I think we've got it."

Angie took that opportunity carry from the kitchen a big Italian hand-painted pasta bowl filled with just-from-the-oven biscotti, amaretti and honey-dipped cookies. The whole thing was wrapped in green cellophane, gathered at the top to form a flowery design and tied with an enormous green ribbon. "Here it is!" she cried.

The old men who were still awake cheered. The others woke from the noise and cheered as well, eventually.

Rebecca knew what she had to do.

She waited for what seemed like a century on the doorstep after speaking with an immaculate butler.

The door reopened and Richie appeared, his gaze questioning.

"I have a present for you," she said and stepped aside.

His expression was indescribable as he saw the twelve Santas, the cookies, and Rebecca. Then his face spread into a wide, toothy smile. "Come on in, guys. Everybody's waiting for you." He stood back, and the Santas entered, single-file, to loud greetings and cheers.

He and Rebecca remained alone in the doorway. "Where'd you find them?" he asked.

She grinned. "They were baking cookies."

Dark eyes met hers. "You've saved my life! Do you realize what the reaction would have been if I told the birthday boy I'd lost his twelve best friends?" He shuddered. "I kept saying they were on their way...and then said three Hail Mary's for it to come true."

She chuckled. "Glad to be of service."

Laughter from the party erupted. In the background, Sinatra sang "Winter Wonderland."

"Rebecca," Richie said, pointedly not using Inspector Mayfield, "come on inside with me. It's Christmas Eve. Join the party."

He took her hand. His was warm, hard and masculine. Thoughts of their crazy adventure filled her, running up and down the streets of Chinatown, him sitting on a curb as she ranted at him, him fighting with Punk Leo in the kitchen.

The air was cool and crisp, the night a velvet canvas filled with stars. Inside were warm lights and happy sounds of the party.

She pulled away her hand. "I don't think so." Once done with work, she'd phone her family in Boise. She wanted to hear and talk to them on this holiest of all nights, a night for families and old, dear friends. She started to turn.

"Maybe some other time?" His eyes were too dark, too difficult for her to read or understand.

"No." She walked down the steps to the sidewalk.

"It's Christmas Eve," he said, hurrying down to her. "Not a time to be alone."

"You've got a party."

"To watch a bunch of people who have spent years together share their memories?" he said wryly. "Maybe I'd rather create some memories of my own, if you don't mind my company."

She kept going, but glanced back at him with a

surprising stab of regret. "Merry Christmas, Richie," she said, unable to hide the warmth in her voice.

She had a job to do, but as she walked to her car, she thought about Santa falling out of his sleigh and chuckled.

"I saw that!" Richie was suddenly at her side again. "See, you really can laugh. Forget the party! You know what? I'm starving. The restaurants are closed, but we can still find beer and pizza someplace and take it over my house. We'll make our own Christmas party."

Everything rational told her to refuse, but another side, a warmer side, told her it was Christmas, a time to share and to forgive...and there was something about Richie Amalfi...

She stopped and faced him. "You know, that idea isn't half bad." And then, despite herself, she smiled.

From the Kitchen of Angelina Amalfi

CHRISTMAS VANILLA HORNS

1 cup (2 sticks) butter –softened
2/3 cup unsifted powdered sugar
1-1/2 tsp vanilla
¾ cup ground pecans
2 cup unsifted all-purpose flour

Beat together butter, sugar and vanilla. Mix well. Add pecans. Stir in flour until well blended. Shape the batter into a ball and place in a bowl covered with wax paper. Refrigerate it one hour.

Preheat oven to 325 degrees. Lightly grease cookie sheets. Measure 1 Tablespoon of dough, roll it into a cylinder, and then bend it to shape it like a crescent moon, and place on cookie sheet.

Continue, using all the batter.

Bake 10-12 minutes until lightly browned. Cool. Dust with powdered sugar.

ANGIE'S EASY RAISIN-BUTTERMILK SODA BREAD

¼ cup white sugar
2 cups all-purpose flour
1 tsp baking powder
½ tsp baking soda
½ tsp salt
½ cup raisins
1 egg
9 oz. buttermilk (OR 1 8-oz carton buttermilk + 1 oz milk, water, or half-and-half)
½ cup sour cream

In a large mixing bowl, combine flour, sugar, baking powder, baking soda, salt, & raisins. Then, in a separate bowl, beat together just until mixed, egg, buttermilk, and sour cream.

Stir the liquid mixture into flour mixture until flour is moistened. Knead the dough in the bowl 10-12 times. The dough will be sticky.

Preheat the oven to 350 degrees.

Place the dough in a greased 9-inch round cake pan or greased cast iron skillet. Allow the dough to rest for at least 20 minutes before cooking it. Dust the top with a sprinkling of flour, and then cut a deep slit in an X- shape on the top of the loaf.

Bake it at 350 degrees for 65-75 minutes, until well browned and bread has a slightly hollow sound when tapped.

BEST LEMON SQUARES EVER

CRUST:

2 cups flour
½ cup powdered sugar
1 cup (2 sticks) butter

Mix, pat and press into 13 x 9 well-greased pan. Bake at 350 degrees for 15 minutes.

TOPPING:

4 eggs
4 Tbs. lemon juice
2 cups sugar
2 Tbs. grated lemon rind
1 Tbs. baking powder
4 Tbs. flour

Beat it all together and pour it over crust. Bake at 350 degrees for 20-25 min. DO NOT OVERBAKE.

Sift powdered sugar on top while hot.

About the Author

Joanne Pence was born and raised in northern California. She has been an award-winning, *USA Today* best-selling author of mysteries for many years, but she has also written suspense, historical fiction, contemporary romance, romantic suspense, and fantasy. All of her books are now available as e-books, and most are also in print.

Joanne hopes you'll enjoy her books, which present a variety of times, places, and reading experiences, from mysterious to thrilling, emotional to lightly humorous, as well as powerful tales of times long past.

Visit her at www.joannepence.com.

Ancient Echoes

Over two hundred years ago, a covert expedition shadowing Lewis and Clark disappeared in the wilderness of Central Idaho. Now, seven anthropology students and their professor vanish in the same area. The key to finding them lies in an ancient secret, one that men throughout history have sought to unveil.

Michael Rempart is a brilliant archeologist with a colorful and controversial career, but he is plagued by a sense of the supernatural and a spiritual intuitiveness. Joining Michael are a CIA consultant on paranormal phenomena, a washed-up local sheriff, and a former scholar of Egyptology. All must overcome their personal demons as they attempt to save the students and learn the expedition's terrible secret.

Seems Like Old Times

When Lee Reynolds, nationally known television news anchor, returns to the small town where she was born to sell her now-vacant childhood home, little does she expect to find that her first love has moved back to town. Nor does she expect that her feelings for him are still so strong.

Tony Santos had been a major league baseball player, but now finds his days of glory gone. He's gone back home to raise his young son as a single dad.

Both Tony and Lee have changed a lot. Yet, being with him, she finds that in her heart, it seems like old times...

Dance With A Gunfighter

Gabriella Devere wants vengeance. She grows up quickly when she witnesses the murder of her family by a gang of outlaws, and vows to make them pay for their crime. When the law won't help her, she takes matters into her own hands.

Jess McLowry left his war-torn Southern home to head West, where he hired out his gun. When he learns what happened to Gabriella's family, and what she plans, he knows a young woman like her will have no chance against the outlaws, and vows to save her the way he couldn't save his own family.

But the price of vengeance is high and Gabriella's willingness to sacrifice everything ultimately leads to the book's deadly and startling conclusion.

This is a harsh and gritty tale of the old West, in the tradition of Charles Portis' *True Grit* and Nancy Turner's *These is My Words*.

The Ghost of Squire House

For decades, the home built by reclusive artist, Paul Squire, has stood empty on a windswept cliff overlooking the ocean. Those who attempted to live in the home soon fled in terror. Jennifer Barrett knows nothing of the history of the house she inherited. All she knows is she's glad for the chance to make a new life for herself.

It's Paul Squire's duty to rid his home of intruders, but something about this latest newcomer's vulnerable status...and resemblance of someone from his past...dulls his resolve. Jennifer would like to find a real flesh-and-blood man to liven her days and nights—someone to share her life with—but living in the artist's house, studying his paintings, she is surprised at how close she feels to him.

A compelling, prickly ghost with a tortured, guilt-ridden past, and a lonely heroine determined to start fresh, find themselves in a battle of wills and emotion in this ghostly fantasy of love, time, and chance.

Gold Mountain

Against the background of San Francisco at the time of the Great Earthquake and Fire of 1906 comes a tale of love and loss. Ruth Greer, wealthy daughter of a shipping magnate, finds a young boy who has run away from his home in Chinatown—an area of gambling parlors, opium dens, sing-song girls, as well as families trying to eke out a living. It is also home to a number of highbinder tongs, the infamous "hatchet men" of Chinese lore.

There, Ruth meets the boy's father, Li Han-lin, the

handsome, enigmatic leader of one such tong, and discovers he is neither as frightening, cruel, or wanton as reputation would have her believe. As Ruth's fascination with the area grows, she finds herself pulled deeper into the intrigue of the lawless area, and Han-lin's life. But the two are from completely different worlds, and when both worlds are shattered by the earthquake and fire that destroys San Francisco, they face their ultimate test.

Dangerous Journey

C.J. Perkins is trying to find her brother who went missing while on a Peace Corps assignment in Asia. All she knows is that the disappearance has something to do with a "White Dragon." Darius Kane, adventurer and bounty hunter, seems to be her only hope, and she practically shanghais him into helping her.

With a touch of the romantic adventure film Romancing the Stone, C.J. and Darius follow a trail that takes them through the narrow streets of Hong Kong, the backrooms of San Francisco's Chinatown, and the wild jungles of Borneo as they pursue both her brother and the White Dragon. The closer C.J. gets to them, the more danger she finds herself in—and it's not just danger of losing her life, but also of losing her heart.

[This is a completely revised author's edition of novel previously published as *Armed and Dangerous*.]

The Angie Amalfi Mysteries

Gourmet cook, sometime food columnist, sometime restaurant critic, and generally "underemployed" person Angelina Amalfi burst upon the mystery scene in SOMETHING'S COOKING, in which she met San Francisco Homicide Inspector Paavo Smith. Since that time—over the course of 14 books and a novella—she's wanted two things in life, a good job...and Paavo.

Here's a brief outline of each book in the order written:

Something's Cooking

For sassy and single food writer Angie Amalfi, life's a banquet—until the man who's been contributing unusual recipes for her food column is found dead. But Angie is hardly one to simper in fear—so instead she simmers over the delectable homicide detective assigned to the case.

Too Many Cooks

Angie is thrilled to have talked her way into a job on a pompous, third-rate chef's radio call-in show. But when a successful and much envied restaurateur is poisoned, Angie finds the case far more interesting than trying to make her pretentious boss sound good.

Cooking Up Trouble

Angie Amalfi's latest job, developing the menu for a new inn, sounds enticing—especially since it means spending a week in scenic Northern California with her homicide-detective boyfriend. But once she arrives at the soon-to-be-opened Hill Haven Inn, she's not so sure anymore. The added ingredients of an ominous treat, a missing person, and a woman making eyes at her man leave Angie convinced that the only recipe in this inn's kitchen is one for disaster.

Cooking Most Deadly

Food columnist Angie Amalfi has it all. But while she's wondering if it's time to cut the wedding cake with her boyfriend, Paavo, he becomes obsessed with a grisly homicide that has claimed two female victims. Angie becomes the next target of a vendetta that stretches from the dining rooms of San Francisco's elite to the seedy Tenderloin.

Cook's Night Out

Angie has decided to make her culinary name by creating the perfect chocolate confection: angelinas. Donating her delicious rejects to a local mission, Angie soon finds that the mission harbors more than the needy, and to save not only her life, but Paavo's as well, she's going to have to discover the truth faster than you can beat egg whites to a peak.

Cooks Overboard

Angie Amalfi's long-awaited vacation with her detective boyfriend has all the ingredients of a romantic getaway—a sail to Acapulco aboard a freighter, no crowds, no Homicide Department worries, and a red bikini. But it isn't long before Angie's *Love Boat* fantasies are headed for stormy seas—the cook tries to jump off the ship, Paavo is acting mighty strange, and someone's added murder to the menu...

A Cook In Time

Angie Amalfi has a way with food and people, but her newest business idea is turning out to be shakier than a fruit-filled gelatin mold. Now, her first—and only—clients for "Fantasy Dinners" are none other than a group of UFO chasers and government conspiracy fanatics. But when it seems that the group has a hidden agenda greater than anything on the *X-Files*, Angie's determined to find out the truth before it takes her out of this world...for good.

To Catch A Cook

Between her latest "sure-fire" foray into the food industry—video restaurant reviews—and her concern over Paavo's depressed state, Angie's plate is full to overflowing. Paavo has never come to terms with the fact that his mother abandoned him when he was four, leaving behind only a mysterious present. But when the token disappears, Angie discovers a lethal goulash of intrigue, betrayal, and mayhem that may spell disaster for her and Paavo.

Bell, Cook, and Candle

For once, Angie's newest culinary venture, "Comical Cakes," seems to be a roaring success! But there's nothing funny about her boyfriend Paavo's latest case—a series of baffling murders that may be rooted in satanic ritual. And it gets harder to focus on pastry alone when strange "accidents" and desecrations to her baked creations begin occurring with frightening regularity—leaving Angie to wonder whether she may end up as devil's food of a different kind.

If Cooks Could Kill

Angie Amalfi's culinary adventures always seem to fall

flat, so now she's decided to cook up something different: love. But her earnest attempts at matchmaking don't go so well—her friend Connie is stood up by a no-show jock. Now Connie's fallen for a tarnished loner, and soon finds herself in the middle of a murder investigation. Angie's determined to find the real killer, but when the trail leads to the kitchen of her favorite restaurant, she fears she's about to discover a family recipe that dishes out disaster...and murder!

Two Cooks A-Killing

Angie hates to leave the side of her hunky fiancé, Paavo, but she gets an offer she can't refuse. She'll be preparing the banquet for her favorite soap opera's reunion special, on the estate where the show was originally filmed! But when a corpse turns up in the mansion's cellar, and Angie starts snooping around to investigate a past on-set death, she discovers that real-life events may be even more theatrical than the soap's on-screen drama.

Courting Disaster

Against her instincts, Angie agrees to let her control-freak mother plan her engagement party—she's just too busy to do it herself. And Angie's even more swamped when murder enters the picture. Now she must follow the trail of a mysterious pregnant kitchen helper at a nearby Greek eatery—a woman who her friendly neighbor Stan is infatuated with. And when Angie gets a little too close to the action, it looks like her fiancé Paavo may end up celebrating solo, after the untimely d.o.a. of his hapless fiancé!

Red Hot Murder

Angie and Paavo have had enough familial input regarding their upcoming wedding to last a lifetime. So Angie leaps at the chance to spend some time with her fiancé in a sun-drenched Arizona town. But when a wealthy local is murdered, uncovering a hotbed of deadly town secrets, Angie's getaway with her lover is starting to look more and more like her final meal.

The DaVinci Cook

Just when dilettante chef Angie Amalfi's checkered culinary career seems to be looking up, she has to drop everything and hightail it to Rome. Her realtor sister is in a stew—accused of murder. To make matters worse, a priceless religious relic is missing as well—so the Amalfi girls are joining forces in the Eternal City...and diving head-first into a simmering cauldron of big trouble.

Cooking Spirits

Angie puts aside her gourmet utensils to concentrate on planning her upcoming wedding. But all her plans pale when she finds the perfect house to share with Paavo, except for one little problem—the house may be haunted. When eerie happenings turn deadly, Angie fears she may be spirited away for good!

o0o

Look for the latest Angie Amalfi mysteries and other books by Joanne Pence by visiting her website at www.joannepence.com.